Barkerville Gold

Barkerville Gold

Dayle Campbell Gaetz

ORCA BOOK PUBLISHERS

National Library of Canada Cataloguing in Publication Data

Gaetz, Dayle, 1947-
Barkerville gold / Dayle Campbell Gaetz.

ISBN 1-55143-306-0

1. Barkerville (B.C.)–History–Juvenile fiction. 2. Cariboo (B.C. :
Regional district)–Gold discoveries–Juvenile fiction. I. Title.

PS8563.A25317B37 2004   C813'.54   C2004-902150-8

Library of Congress Control Number: 2004105087

Summary: Rusty, Katie and Sheila journey to historic Barkerville where they
become involved in a search for missing gold.

Orca Book Publishers gratefully acknowledges the support for its
publishing programs provided by the following agencies:
the Government of Canada through the Book Publishing Industry Development
Program (BPIDP), the Canada Council for the Arts, and the British Columbia Arts
Council.

Cover design by Lynn O'Rourke
Cover illustration by Ljuba Levstek

In Canada:
ORCA BOOK PUBLISHERS
BOX 5626 STN.B
VICTORIA, BC CANADA
V8R 6S4

In the United States:
ORCA BOOK PUBLISHERS
PO Box 468
CUSTER, WA USA
98240-0468

08 07 06 05 04 • 6 5 4 3 2 1

Printed and bound in Canada

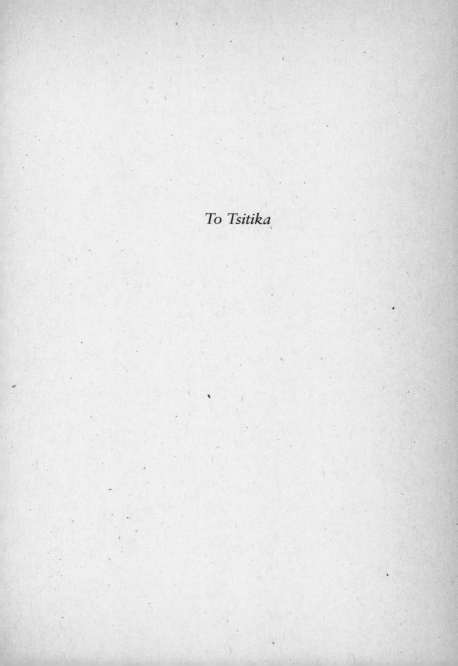

To Tsitika

1

Run Out of Town

Rusty squeezed farther into the corner and stared gloomily out the narrow window beside him. He wished he was somewhere else, anywhere but squished into the backseat of his grandparents' crew-cab truck. Okay, he did want to see Barkerville—but not like this, with these two girls for company. He glanced sideways at Sheila. She looked like some weird visitor from deep space. Bright yellow earphones stuck out from each side of her freckled face, and the headpiece squashed her short, honey-gold hair, making it poke out like horns above her eyes. Sheila's head bobbed up and down in time to rock music no one else could hear. Music, sports and animals—that was all Sheila cared about.

Rusty leaned forward to see Katie, her nose buried in yet another mystery novel, and a small, exasperated groan escaped his lips. So what if his cousin solved one stupid mystery last week? Did that make her some big detective?

Katie turned a page and noticed Rusty staring at her. She wrinkled her brow, narrowed her dark brown eyes in warning and returned to her book.

Instead of the fun visit he and his parents had planned, this was going to be torture. Katie and Sheila didn't want him tagging along any more than he wanted to be here. He sighed and turned back to the window. A small stream ran beside the road. Beyond it was a forest of firs and pines that seemed small and stunted compared to the towering conifers Rusty was used to on the coast. Above the trees a broad-winged bird soared against a background of pure blue sky. A hawk? An eagle? A raven? Rusty had no idea. Sheila would know, but he couldn't be bothered asking her.

He tried to imagine something worse than being stuck in a truck with a music-loving, athletic, wildlife nut and a self-appointed brilliant detective. *Jamie Sloan*. The name slid into his brain and made his stomach twist. *Jamie the Jock*, the kid who made Rusty dread going to school every single day. Jamie saw to it that Rusty was last to be chosen for every team in every gym class. *Rusty Geek*, Jamie called him, instead of Rusty Gates. *Rusty Geek likes history better than hockey.*

Which wasn't true. Maybe he couldn't play very well, but Rusty loved watching hockey on TV. So what if he loved history too? Was that a crime? His dad worked at the archives and kept coming home with fascinating stories from the past. His mom wrote about history in books and magazines and often had a funny history story to share at the dinner table. Which is why, for the past year, Rusty and his parents had been planning a trip to the restored gold-rush town of Barkerville. They read everything they could find about it, shared stories about some of the weird characters who once lived there, and looked forward to exploring the little town together.

How could they do this to him?

Rusty drummed his fingers on the armrest. It wasn't fair the way his parents ganged up with Katie's parents and Sheila's mom to send the three of them out of town for the entire summer. *For your own safety,* they said. Yeah, right.

The really annoying thing was—they had no good reason.

Well, okay, maybe one small reason if you count almost getting themselves killed in the first few days of summer holidays. But, hey, it's not like they were planning to do that every week. Besides, hadn't they outwitted the bad guys and brought them to justice? They should be treated like heroes. "You aren't supposed to run the good guys out of town," Rusty said, but his voice was overpowered by the hourly news blasting out of the truck radio.

Rusty's fingers drummed harder against the armrest. He was sick of sitting here with no one to talk to and nothing to see but trees, the back of a bucket seat and one monster yellow earphone. Nothing to listen to but CBC Radio. His mind strayed to the book his parents had given him just before he left home. Rusty had been so mad he refused to look at it. But now he leaned forward and pulled the large book from his backpack on the floor.

He studied the black-and-white photograph on the front cover. It showed a narrow dirt road, the original Cariboo Wagon Road, with a stagecoach being pulled by six powerful horses whose hooves stirred up a cloud of dust. *Barnard's Express* was written on the stagecoach door.

Standing beside the road, just ahead of the stage, was a ragged-looking man. He was bone thin, with a bushy beard and a wild look in his eyes. His flat-topped hat was falling apart, his thin jacket full of holes, and his pants ripped and torn. Even the man's boots gaped open at the toes. He leaned heavily on a crooked walking stick with one hand, but held the other outstretched, palm upward, toward the approaching stagecoach, as if begging for money. The really weird thing was that you could almost, but not completely, see right through this man, as if he weren't quite there at all.

Rusty ran his fingers over the book's title, printed in tall, wobbly letters. *"Spirits of the Cariboo,"* he whispered, "by I.B. Spectre." The spine creaked as Rusty opened the book for the very first time and an inky-papery smell filled his nostrils. When he turned to the table of contents, one title practically leaped off the page at him "Barkerville's Most Notorious Ghost." He turned to page 52.

2

Three Finger's Story

Barkerville's Most Notorious Ghost
I.B. Spectre

James Evans was born in Cornwall, Ontario, on
September 17, 1826. In 1856, at the age of thirty,
he married Emily McTavish and the couple settled
down to live and work together on his family's farm.
In 1859, they had a son who they named James,
after his father.

Evans was a small thin man who worked hard but
tended to be rather clumsy.

Just like me, Rusty thought and wondered if James Evans was clumsy for the same reason: because he couldn't
stop daydreaming. He turned back to the book.

All his life Evans had one accident after another,
most of them insignificant. In the autumn of 1862,
however, while cutting firewood for the winter, he

managed to chop two fingers off his left hand. The injury took a long time to heal, and even after it did, Evans had difficulty doing many of the chores required of a farmer.

In 1864 he met John "Cariboo" Cameron, who had just returned from the Cariboo, bringing the bodies of his wife, Sophia, who died in Barkerville, and their small daughter, who died in Victoria. Cameron had promised Sophia he would bury them both at home. In spite of his terrible losses, Cariboo Cameron had struck it rich and would never need to farm again. Talking with Cameron set Evans to thinking.

That same year, Evans left his wife, young son and newborn daughter at home and set off for the Cariboo. He promised to send for his family when he was a wealthy man, likely by the following spring.

Unfortunately, by the time Evans arrived in Barkerville, all of the rich gold-bearing claims were already staked. To make matters worse, the loose placer gold available in sand and gravel was gone. Any remaining gold was buried deep underground and to mine it required expensive equipment for digging shafts and tunnels. So James Evans ended up working for others. Almost inevitably he became known as "Three Finger" Evans.

Although he wrote often to Emily, as hard as he worked, Three Finger could not earn enough money to send for her. In fact, he didn't even have enough to pay his own way home. This was partly because Three Finger kept having one mishap after another.

In the winter of 1865, he got caught in a blizzard overnight and, as a result, lost three toes to frostbite.

They must have called him "Three Finger–Two Toe" after that, Rusty thought, and he read on to find out what other appendages James Evans lost.

In the spring of 1867, Three Finger was limping around in the dark of night when he tumbled into an abandoned mine shaft. Luckily for him it had been partially filled in with dirt, so the shaft was fairly shallow and contained no water at the bottom. Three Finger was not killed, but because the shaft was high on the hillside above Stout's Gulch, no one heard his cries for help. He spent a long night at the bottom of the shaft with a broken leg.

Suddenly Rusty was there. Falling, falling down and down into a cold, dark, underground shaft. He was stuck, unable to move. He made a sound in his throat, almost a scream. Then he shuddered and tried to push aside the memory. He returned to the book.

The next morning, Evans' friend, Kees van der Boorg, tracked him down and helped get him out. But Three Finger's leg never healed properly. For the remainder of his life, he limped badly.

Three Finger–Two Toe–Gimpy Leg, Rusty thought. The man's name kept getting longer. What else could Evans do to himself?

Three Finger began to age quickly. His hair turned completely gray and began to fall out. Over the next year and a half, rumors started to spread. Miners and mine owners noticed that, slowly but steadily, gold nuggets were disappearing from one mine after another. Every time this happened, Chinese workers were blamed and immediately fired.

However, recently discovered old account books reveal something no one appeared to notice at the time. Every time a mine had problems with theft, Three Finger Evans was on the payroll.

In the spring of 1868, Three Finger told van der Boorg he was determined to return home that year no matter what. Although he worked hard all summer, Three Finger was slower than bigger, stronger, younger men who had ten fingers, ten toes and two good legs. He earned scarcely enough money to buy food and clothing for himself. Van der Boorg could not believe his friend would ever earn enough money to buy his passage home.

On September 10, 1868, a story appeared in the *Cariboo Sentinel*. It stated: "One well-known mine owner has accused a certain James 'Three Finger' Evans of pilfering a fortune in gold, a few nuggets at a time, hidden carefully within his undergarments. He threatened to run Evans out of town."

Oh, man! Rusty thought. *Run out of town, just like me.* He was beginning to feel a certain kinship with Three Finger Evans.

A few days later, the *Cariboo Sentinel* published another story telling of unsolved crimes: "On the nights of September 12, 13 and 14, an odd assortment of items disappeared from various establishments around town. The first night, two bottles of Hair Invigorator were taken from W.D. Moses' barbershop; the next, three bottles of whiskey vanished from Barry and Adler's Saloon; on the third night, four leather pouches for carrying gold bullion disappeared from Mason and Daly General Merchants."

Some folks began to view Three Finger with suspicion. His hair definitely needed invigorating, he certainly enjoyed his whiskey, and if he stole all that gold, wouldn't he need something to put it in? However, most people, without any real evidence to back them up, blamed a young Chinese man, Eng Quan, who was often seen walking the streets at night and so could very well have robbed the stores.

This is too cool, Rusty thought and put down the book. Katie was still concentrating on her mystery novel and he wanted to tell her that here, in his book, was a real live mystery to solve. But he couldn't say anything now, with their grandparents in the front seat, not after they had promised not to worry Gram and GJ by getting involved in another mystery. He picked up the book again.

On the afternoon of September 16, 1868, Three Finger was at Barry and Adler's Saloon along with the usual crowd of miners and "Hurdy Gurdy," or dancing, girls. Three Finger told van der Boorg that he had finally saved up enough money to go home. "My backpack is ready, loaded with enough food and drink for the trail and stashed behind my outhouse where no one's likely to steal it. Tonight, at midnight, I'm leaving this town forever."

No one knows exactly what happened that day, but the story goes that a miner, trying to force a Hurdy Gurdy girl to kiss him, bumped against the woodstove and knocked a hot pipe against the canvas ceiling. In minutes the saloon was ablaze. Flames leaped across the street and quickly spread through the town, which was built entirely of wood, tinder dry after a long drought.

People scrambled to gather their possessions, which they placed in Williams Creek. Then someone remembered that fifty kegs of blasting powder were sitting in a store, and everyone rushed to move them into a dry shaft so they would not explode.

In slightly over an hour it was all over. No one was hurt, but the lower part of town was destroyed. When people returned to retrieve their meager possessions from the creek, they discovered that even as the fire raged, someone had crept in and gone through their belongings. Gold nuggets they had carefully saved were missing. Most blamed the Chinese who lived in the upper town, scarcely touched by the fire.

But a few miners, facing a long cold night with no shelter and few blankets to keep them warm, got to talking. They decided that Three Finger was a likely culprit.

They drank some whiskey to help keep warm and talked some more. Hidden by darkness, van der Boorg heard all of this and sneaked off to warn his friend. By moonlight he climbed the trail northwest of Barkerville, up toward Lowhee Creek, and arrived at the cabin long before midnight. Finding no sign of Three Finger, van der Boorg hoped he had already left town. He made his way to the outhouse and was dismayed to find Three Finger's backpack behind it. That's when he heard familiar voices. The angry miners had come after Three Finger. Clutching the pack, van der Boorg disappeared into the woods.

Next morning, when Three Finger did not show up, van der Boorg searched down mine shafts, at the bottom of the canyon, throughout the sur-rounding woods and finally inside the outhouse, but Three Finger had disappeared, never to be seen alive again.

However, one of the leather pouches stolen from Mason and Daly's was found half buried under the back stairs of the apothecary shop owned by Eng Chung, the father of Eng Quan. The pouch con-tained traces of gold dust.

Three Finger was instantly forgotten, and blame shifted back to Eng Quan, who lived with his elderly father above the apothecary shop. When miners went to find him, Eng Quan was gone. His broken body was later found at the base of a cliff.

It is probable that Three Finger also perished in the rugged terrain surrounding Barkerville. Without supplies, unable to show his face on the road, even an expert woodsman didn't stand much of a chance. And Three Finger was no expert.

For years men searched for the gold, believing that whichever man stole it, he must have buried it in a safe place until he was ready to leave town. However, it was never recovered.

Soon after Three Finger's disappearance, some folks began to see, at midnight, a small thin man wearing a wide-brimmed hat, bandanna, vest, plaid shirt, pants and heavy boots limp his solitary way between Stout's Gulch Trail and the Lowhee Trail. Even today, he is occasionally spotted on moonlit nights, at midnight. Perhaps James Evans is still searching for his fortune in gold so that he can finally go home.

"We're here!" GJ called out. He slowed the truck and steered onto a narrow road leading into a provincial campground. "Keep your eyes peeled for a good campsite."

Rusty read the wooden sign near the gate: *Lowhee Campground.* He closed his book.

3

A Ghost at Midnight

After dinner that evening, Rusty settled outside on a folding chair to sketch Three Finger Evans. He started with the hat: round, flat top, wide brim.

"Do you want to play Crazy Eights with us?" Gram asked.

Rusty looked up. His grandmother held a pack of cards, and everyone was gathering around the picnic table. He closed his sketchbook and joined them.

It was sometime during the game, when they were all guzzling ice water, munching potato chips and complaining about the heat, that Rusty got the idea. "Can we pitch our tents out here tonight?" he asked. "It's way too hot to sleep inside the trailer."

Gram and GJ looked at each other and both nodded at once. But GJ turned to Rusty with a stern look. "Be sure you don't take any food into your tent. I mean nothing. No potato chips, no chocolate bars, no apples, nothing."

15

"Hey, why look at me? Tell that to Katie and Sheila."

"You're the walking stomach," Katie reminded him, "not me."

"No food in any tent," GJ said firmly. "Unless, of course, you want to attract bears."

Bears? Rusty swallowed. He opened his backpack and removed the pile of chocolate chip cookies and half bag of barbecue-flavored potato chips he had been saving for emergencies. But GJ held out his hand.

"Oh, man!" Rusty fished around in the bottom and pulled out a big chocolate bar. "It's still wrapped. How's a bear supposed to smell it?"

"You'd be surprised," Sheila told him. "Bears might not have very good eyesight, but they can sniff out a chocolate bar from miles away."

At first they considered pitching their little one-person tents in a far corner of the campsite, near the trees. But with thoughts of black bears lurking in all of their minds, they ended up pitching them side by side in a neat row between the trailer and picnic table.

"We'll close only the screen door," Gram said as they dragged foamies out to their tents, "so if you need anything, you can slip inside."

By the time it was almost dark, they were anxious to try out their tents for the first time.

"I'm going to listen to music," Sheila said, unzipping the flap on her tent, "so if you two are talking and I don't answer, you'll know why."

"We won't be talking." Katie, on her knees, was already half into the middle tent, her mystery novel tucked under one arm. "I want to finish my book. I think I know who did it."

"Who did what?" Rusty asked.

"You'll have to read the book," Katie called from inside. The zipper gave a high-pitched squeal as she zipped her door closed.

Rusty dragged his backpack into his tent and pulled out his ghost book, sketchbook and pencils. There was enough room to sit on his mattress and just enough light to see. With his sketchbook balanced on both knees, Rusty set to work. First he drew a bearded face below the wide-brimmed hat. Then he added a plaid shirt, vest and three-fingered hand. He gave the man short legs covered by loose-fitting pants that wrinkled at the knees and tucked into high boots. His sketch was similar to the drawing in the book, but he placed Three Finger walking instead of crouched over a gold pan.

Rusty skimmed quickly through the Three Finger Evans story again, in an effort to pick out any details he may have missed, things he could add to his drawing. He decided to draw a bottle of Hair Invigorator in Three

Finger's good hand, but when he turned back to his sketch he had difficulty seeing it in the fading light. He lay down on his stomach and inched forward to hold his sketchbook as close as possible to the mesh door, then sketched a bottle into Three Finger's good hand.

Yawning, Rusty put down his pencil and looked outside. Everything was in shades of gray now, and the outlines of trees were black against the starlit sky; the short stretch of road in front of the campsite shone silvery white in the moonlight. He yawned again, tucked the sketchbook under his pillow and rolled onto his back. Thousands of stars, so bright overhead, seemed closer here than they ever did at home. His eyes closed.

Rusty didn't know what woke him up. It could not have been the sound of footsteps because they were so faint he was not even aware of them until after he saw the ghost.

Whatever it was, something made him open his eyes. When he did, he was facing a triangle of mesh doorway, several shades lighter than the tent walls surrounding it. From the corner of his eye, Rusty caught a hint of movement out on the road. He lifted his head from the pillow. His eyes grew huge and he gasped softly. He held his breath.

A lone figure on the silvery road stood out clearly against the dark trees. It was a small thin man wearing a

18

wide-brimmed hat pulled low over his eyes. Although the colors were indistinct, his full beard shone white beneath the moon, and Rusty saw that he wore a bandanna, shirt, vest and pants tucked into boots that reached almost to his knees. He carried something in his left hand, on the far side of his body. Rusty could not make out exactly what it was, but it looked like a large cloth bag with something heavy inside. The man hurried along the road past the campsite.

Rusty's heart thudded against his ribs. Its quick *thump-thump-thump* mingled with the soft *puff, puff, puff* of footsteps on dust. When the man disappeared from sight, Rusty pressed the little button on his watch and its face lit up: 12:00. Midnight. A chill ran up his spine.

He turned toward Katie's tent, next to his, and was relieved to see a faint glow, right through the nylon of his own tent. Trust her to still be reading at this hour.

"Katie!" he tried to call, but his voice caught somewhere in his throat and all that emerged was a faint squeak. He swallowed. *Okay*, he told himself, *don't panic. Do not panic. Think this through.* Rusty took a deep breath and counted on his fingers:

1. Midnight.
2. The man from his book.
3. The same man he sketched before falling asleep.

4. His voice refused to work.

5. This was his last finger.

Obviously he was dreaming, and there was one sure way to prove it. He pinched himself on the cheek, just below his eye. Hard. "Ouch!" That really hurt! Which could only mean...

"Rusty? What's going on?"

Oh, man! Katie had heard him. "Nothing."

"You okay? Why did you say *ouch*?"

"I'm fine." He hesitated, but had to ask. "Did you see the ghost?"

"Huh?"

"The ghost, did you see it walk by?"

"You mean that old guy dressed like a prospector from the gold rush?"

"So you did see it!"

"I saw a man. I didn't see a ghost. How many times do I have to tell you I don't believe in ghosts?"

Rusty couldn't think of an answer.

"So—why did you say he was a ghost?"

"C'mon outside," he said, "and bring your flashlight. I'll show you."

They sat at the picnic table and spoke in whispers.

Rusty handed Katie his sketch. She shone her flashlight on it and studied it for a moment. "Good drawing," she said. "It looks just like him. But I don't know why you dragged me out here to see it. I already know you're good at drawing people."

"Katie, don't you see? I drew that *before* he walked past! And look at this." He shoved *Spirits of the Cariboo* across the picnic table toward her, open to the story of Three Finger Evans. "This is a brand-new book, just published."

"Rusty, I only have two pages left in my mystery. I don't want to read something else right now."

"But you have to. It's important. Look at the little picture in the corner."

Katie shone her light on the drawing, then on Rusty's sketch, then on the photograph again. She started to read. Rusty drummed his fingers on the table and watched his cousin until she finally looked up. "That old guy fits the description perfectly."

Rusty nodded.

Katie switched off her flashlight and jumped up. "Let's go!"

Rusty grinned to himself. He had no idea where they were going, but he didn't much care. All it took was a hint of suspicion, the smallest suggestion of mystery, and his cousin would be hooked. She would never want to leave Barkerville until she solved it.

4

Dusty Prints

On this cloudless, northern summer night there was enough light to clearly see where they were going as Rusty followed his cousin toward the road. He had no idea why she stopped suddenly at the edge of the road and switched on her flashlight, so he kept on walking.

"Stop!" Katie whispered and grabbed his shirt.

"Why?"

"Look!" Her flashlight shot a bright oval onto the dusty road.

Katie crept onto the road, stopped and directed the beam straight down. Rusty followed. Spotlighted in the dust was a perfect print. An unusual print. Not an animal print; not made by a sandal or a sneaker or a bare foot; the tread pattern was very different from anything Rusty had seen before.

"Do ghosts usually leave footprints?" Katie whispered.

He shook his head. "No. I don't know. Who knows?"

"Trust me, they don't." Katie straightened up. "We need a picture of this. I wish we had a camera."

"Stay here, I'll get my sketchbook." Rusty ran to the picnic table, grabbed his sketchbook and pencil and hurried back.

Katie held the light steady on the print while Rusty crouched to make a sketch of it. When he was done he ripped off a clean sheet of paper and laid it beside the print to measure its exact length and width.

"What's going on here?" a voice croaked.

Rusty froze. Someone was standing in the shadows near the entrance to their campsite. Katie swung around and shone the light on the dark figure. A pale face appeared. A pale, freckled face. Sheila squinted, rubbed her eyes and yawned. Her hair shone like gold but stuck out in a great lump to one side. Like Katie and Rusty she wore shorts, a T-shirt and sandals.

"Nothing's going on," Rusty said.

"Shh!" Katie warned.

"Okay," Sheila cleared her throat, lowered her voice, "so I wake up and see a flashlight switch on and off. I look out and there's Rusty running to the picnic table. He grabs his sketchbook and runs back to the road. Now he's hunched down, in the middle of the road, in the middle of the night, laying a piece of paper in the dust. And you tell me *nothing's going on?*" Her voice rose.

23

"Shhh," Katie said.

"I'm just sketching a footprint," Rusty explained, as if it were a perfectly normal thing to be doing at this hour.

"Oh, no!" Sheila backed away. "You better not be starting some big mystery thing again. I promised my mom I wouldn't cause any trouble for your grandparents and I'm not going to break my promise."

"No problem," Katie assured her. "Just go on back to bed. You don't need to get involved." She turned to Rusty. "How's it going?"

"Not that good," he whispered. "It's hard to get the exact size unless I put the paper half over the print."

"Then do it. You've already made your sketch, so it doesn't matter if you wipe out the print."

Rusty held the thin sheet of paper over the footprint. If he laid it down the center, he could mark the length between toe and heel on his paper. But he would rather have a complete outline of the print.

"Wait!" Sheila said.

He held the paper still.

"The police would make a plaster cast so they'd have an exact copy of the footprint."

"Good idea." Sheila's mom was a police officer, so she should know. "I'm guessing you have some plaster of Paris in your tent?"

"Even if she did," Katie whispered, "it wouldn't work.

This is just dry dust. You need something solid to make a mold—like clay or thick mud."

With a soft grunt Rusty pushed himself to his feet.

"Could we, like, make some mud?" Sheila suggested. Just down the road in front of the washrooms, a silver water tap, set into a wooden post, gleamed in the moonlight like an invitation.

"Right," Rusty said, "we'll just dump a bucket of water on it."

They all stared down at a footprint so fragile it threatened to vanish in the faintest breeze.

"Hey! I have an idea!" Sheila's voice burst out so loudly she paused, glanced quickly around and continued in a whisper. "You two walk along the road and look for the clearest print you can find. I'll be right back." She ran toward her tent.

"What's she doing?" Rusty asked.

"Who knows?" Katie started in the direction of the tap, sweeping her flashlight back and forth across the road as she went.

Rusty ran to catch up. They walked side by side, bent low, noses close over the ground. But the footprints had disappeared. Beyond the comforting beam of Katie's flashlight, every black shadow beneath every dark tree took on a sinister appearance. Rusty shuddered. "This must be where he vanished into thin air!"

"Look at this." Katie pointed at the road.

Rusty looked down at another print, a little deeper and clearer than the first, but with the same distinctive tread. It was directly in front of the water tap, where the dirt was dampened by spray from people filling up their bottles and cooking pots during the day.

"I'm guessing your ghost reappeared right here," Katie remarked.

Before Rusty could think of a suitable reply, Sheila joined them, carrying something white and cylindrical in one hand.

"Let's try this." She bent to spray a fine mist over the print.

"Ugh!" Rusty covered his nose. "That stinks! What is it?"

"Hair spray."

"Hair spray! You're using hair spray to catch a ghost?"

"It hardens like rock in just a few minutes," Sheila explained, patting her stiff hair.

"Besides, it isn't a ghost we're after," Katie reminded him. "It's a man."

They waited. Sheila touched the edges of the footprint, then sprayed it again. They waited some more. After a fourth spraying, Sheila finally said, "Okay, now lay that paper on top, gently, and see if you can get a rubbing."

The print had hardened as if it was coated with glue. Rusty laid his thin sheet of clean white paper over it and rubbed gently with the side of his pencil. Slowly, an indistinct image appeared on the paper in front of him. Far from a perfect imprint, it at least provided a rough outline of the sole.

"By the way," Sheila said as they headed back to their campsite, "just wondering. Why are we doing this?"

Rusty waited for Katie to explain, but when she didn't answer he felt obligated to offer an explanation of his own. "Because," he said and left it at that. Because, if he stopped to think about it, he really had no idea why they did it. He only knew that it seemed like a good idea at the time.

"Because you never know," Katie explained patiently, "when you might need proof."

"Yeah? Of what?"

"You never know," Katie repeated wisely.

"Just remember, I'm not getting involved in any mystery," Sheila said, "at least not anything dangerous. I promised."

"No problem." Katie dropped to her knees in front of her tent. "I've got to make some notes," she said and crawled inside.

"There is no mystery," Rusty assured Sheila. "Nothing but a quiet little ghost wandering around in the night and leaving his footprints in the dust." He tucked the loose paper back into his sketchbook and slid the book under his pillow. Then he crawled inside his tent. The air was much cooler now, so he pulled his sleeping bag up and over his shoulders. The pillow felt good, soft and cool beneath his head. He closed his eyes and thought about Three Finger Evans and the missing gold and the ghost.

That's when he heard it. The soft padding of footsteps. Rusty propped himself up on one elbow. Moonlight no longer fell on the road, and the high, ragged wall of trees loomed even blacker now beneath a dome of starlit sky. But out there, on the pale gray road, someone was walking. Rusty could see well enough to recognize Three Finger's ghost. He walked surprisingly quickly now, scurrying along in the opposite direction from before. This time, though, he was empty-handed.

Rusty waited until long after the footfalls had faded to nothing, then called out softly, "Did you see it?" But no one answered. "Katie?" he called a little louder. Still no answer.

He covered his head with his sleeping bag and was just drifting off to sleep when he heard something. Not footsteps, but a cough. A gruff, wheezy sort of cough. Rusty's eyes popped open. He shook his head free of the sleeping bag and rolled over to look outside. All Rusty could see of the shadowy figure was the profile of a wide-brimmed hat and a full white beard that showed up in the faint light of stars.

In spite of Katie's skepticism, Rusty thought this really was the ghost of Three Finger Evans. And he must be getting tired by now—*do ghosts get tired?*—because, in spite of the darkness, Rusty could see that the ghost stooped forward from the waist and his long arms hung down like a chimpanzee's.

"Katie! Sheila!" he called as loudly as he dared. When no one answered, he settled back quietly on his pillow, watching the road, half expecting Three Finger to walk past again and again and again, all night long, night after night, still searching for his fortune in stolen gold.

5

Wake-Up Jake

Before eight o'clock the next morning, they all donned backpacks and climbed on their bikes to ride the short distance into Barkerville. Katie seemed lost in thought and Sheila was unusually quiet. Rusty could scarcely contain his excitement.

After locking their bikes outside the Visitors' Center, they stopped to gaze up at a gigantic wood carving of Billy Barker. The old prospector was crouched down, clutching a gold pan in both hands. With his bushy beard and wide-brimmed hat, Barker looked a lot like the man Rusty had seen in the night.

Rusty pulled his sketchbook from his backpack and opened it to his "ghost" sketch. He pulled out a pencil and studied the serious expression on Billy Barker's face. If this man hadn't left England and traveled halfway around the world to Williams Creek in 1862, if he hadn't ignored what everyone told him and chosen a rocky outcrop below the canyon because he believed an old creek once ran through there and deposited gold, and if he hadn't constructed a shafthouse and dug and dug and kept on digging while all the other miners made fun of him, then he never would have struck gold at fifty-two feet below ground, and the town of Barkerville would not have grown around Barker's claim. "It's hard to believe he lost all his money and died penniless in Victoria," Rusty said, but no one answered.

He glanced around. *Where did everybody go?* Then he spotted them, just entering the Visitors' Center. He ran to catch up.

"Hurry up, Rusty," Gram called, waiting at the door. "Please try to pay attention and keep up with us."

She sounded a lot like his mother, except more polite. Rusty wondered how long that would last. Last summer, it took three days before she lost her patience with him. But it wasn't his fault. He couldn't help getting interested in stuff.

Stepping onto the dusty main street of Barkerville was like stepping into a time warp. The narrow street was lined on both sides with wood-frame structures, false-fronted buildings that looked like the setting for an old cowboy movie. On their left a man was hitching horses to a shiny red wagon with the words *Barnard's Express* written on its side. After they passed Saint Saviour's Church, Rusty stopped to look back. The church faced down the length of Barkerville's main street as if keeping a watchful eye on everything that happened. He had seen so many pictures of it, the church seemed like an old friend, with vertical wood siding, steeply pitched roof and a small steeple perched at the peak.

Barkerville was quiet at this hour, as if it had yet to wake up. Rusty wandered past the schoolhouse and pressed his nose against the dark window of Cameron and Ames Blacksmith Shop. He wanted to see everything, do everything and experience everything. But first, he really needed food. "I'm hungry!" he said.

Again no one answered. *Now where did they go?*

"You coming, Rusty?" Across the street, on the raised plank sidewalk, Gram waited outside a small old-fashioned house with a gabled roof and white wood siding. Above the unusually high and narrow door were the words WAKE-UP JAKE.

Rusty recognized the name. It came from a miner named Jake who used to fall asleep there every morning before his breakfast arrived. Rusty ran across the street, drawn as much by history as the smell of fresh-brewed coffee and sizzling bacon. He charged up the steps two at a time and had almost reached the boardwalk when it suddenly occurred to him that this authentic gold-rush restaurant might serve only authentic gold-rush meals: bacon, beans and biscuits, the staple diet back in gold-rush days. Food was very expensive then because it had to be carried by steamer and pack horses all the way from Victoria. Thinking of this, Rusty stumbled, missed the top step, lurched forward, caught himself, grinned at Gram and eased past her through the open door.

"Try to stay with us, Rusty," Gram sighed, snatching his baseball cap as he went by, "and watch where you're going!"

So, Rusty thought, *no more "please."* Now his grandmother sounded *exactly* like his mother. And they had left Victoria only two days ago. A new personal best.

He plunked himself onto a chair between GJ and Sheila. Gram hung his red baseball cap on the back, and he slipped his sketchbook under the placemat, just in case he felt the urge to draw something in a hurry. He snatched up a menu. "What a relief!" he said. "They have real food here."

Someone laughed. He glanced up. And his jaw almost hit his collarbone. A waitress, holding a full pot of coffee, hovered close above him. Her chestnut-colored hair was braided at the nape of her neck and she wore a long blue-and-white-checkered dress. Perfect white teeth, laughing brown eyes. *Wow!*

"We may look as though we're back in the 1870s," she said, "but trust me, our food is completely modern. And it's really good too!"

Rusty watched her pour coffee for his grandparents. "I'll give you a few minutes to decide what you want," she said and winked at him before she hurried away.

"Hey! Look at Rusty," Katie said in a voice that filled the room. "His face is redder than his hair." She grinned, leaned closer to Sheila and whispered something. Both girls laughed.

Rusty felt his face turn even redder.

They ate their way through huge stacks of thick, fluffy pancakes floating in maple syrup and butter.

"Do you think that will last you until lunchtime?" GJ asked.

Rusty grinned and patted his belly. "Hope so!"

"Wanna bet he'll be hungry in an hour?" Katie asked.

Rusty glared at the back of her head as Katie hurried outside to join Sheila. The girls stood side by side on the plank sidewalk, squinting against a cloud of dry dust that blew in their faces from the road several feet below.

Rusty followed his grandparents outside. A woman strolled toward them along the boardwalk, wearing a green wide-skirted dress that hid her feet. Perched jauntily on top of her head was a small hat. She nodded politely as she passed. Rusty raised his hand to lift his baseball cap, just a touch, like a gentleman from the old days. But his head was bare. What happened to his baseball cap?

The woman crossed the street and nodded at two men lounging in front of the Goldfield Bakery. Both men raised their hats politely. Rusty wished he had a hat like theirs. Not cowboy hats exactly, they were smaller and flatter on top with narrower brims. In fact, they looked a lot like the hat in his ghost sketch.

He looked for his sketchbook. Where was it? Oh, man! He had been in Barkerville for less than an hour and had already lost two things. No wonder he drove other people crazy. He drove himself crazy too.

Rusty shrugged off his backpack, crouched down and dumped the contents onto the boardwalk. Water bottle, Swiss Army knife, a crunchy gray sock that used to be white and the old maps his father gave him. No cap. No sketchbook.

Wait. Okay, now he remembered. The sketchbook was tucked under his arm when he walked into Wake-Up Jake's, and he slipped it under his placemat. He scooped his stuff into his backpack and darted into the restaurant.

Two men sat at the table Rusty and the others had just left, both facing away from him. He spotted his red baseball cap hanging on the chair now occupied by a husky man with sandy-colored hair that curled over his collar. The man beside him looked small in comparison. He was thin with very short, absolutely straight black hair. Both men wore tan short-sleeved shirts above tan-colored jeans.

The big man's muscular arms rested on the placemat. Rusty grabbed his cap, plopped it backward on his head and peeked over the man's shoulder. He gulped when he spotted a book lying on the table. *Spirits of the Cariboo* by I.B. Spectre.

But his sketchbook. Was it still there, under the placemat, lodged beneath those two big hairy arms? Rusty raised up on his toes, leaned forward and tried to see. Impossible. So he reached his hand, fingers outstretched, to tap on the man's shoulder. He paused when he noticed a gray badge on the man's sleeve. On it, the word *Security* was printed in clear, gold letters.

"It's anyone's guess where that gold ended up. For my money, I'm betting Eng Quan made off with it," said the big man.

Rusty froze, still leaning toward the man, arm outstretched and weight balanced on the toes of one foot. But he didn't dare move because he wanted to hear what these men had to say. They must have read the same story he did, about Three Finger, Eng Quan and the missing gold.

The smaller man shook his head. "I don't think Eng Quan had anything to do with the theft. Sounds to me like he was set up by Evans."

"I dunno, Dave. Either way, though, thanks to this book, we can expect to be overrun with folks searching for that missing gold this summer. It's amazing how a new story like this can come out after all this time, but it means we have to work quickly to find the gold before..."

Suddenly everything fell apart. Someone tapped Rusty's arm. He lost his balance and his outstretched hand landed heavily on the big man's shoulder. Which might not have been so bad if the man hadn't just picked up a very full mug of hot black coffee.

"What the—" The man's chair crashed over backward as he leapt up. He whirled around, wiping frantically at the dark wet patch on the front of his pants.

"Sorry," Rusty murmured. And decided to make a hasty retreat. He stepped quickly back and landed on something soft. A toe.

"Ow!"

He swung around and came face to face with the waitress. The beautiful waitress with the great smile. Only she was not smiling now. Her face was scrunched up in pain. "Nice work!" she said and thrust his sketchbook at him.

"Sorry," he gulped.

Grabbing a large jug of ice water, the waitress scurried past him. "Hold still!" she yelled and tossed the water at the man's steaming pants.

"I'm sorry!" Rusty offered for the third time, but no one heard. So he tucked his sketchbook under his arm, scuttled for the door and almost collided with someone coming in. Rusty gaped. The man wore a red-and-black-checked shirt, brown vest and brown pants tucked into high leather boots. Pale gray eyes studied him from under bushy eyebrows that blended into scraggly gray hair and a full white beard. In his right hand was a wide-brimmed hat.

Rusty's eyes dropped to the sketchbook he was holding. The man's eyes followed, saw the ghost sketch and jerked back to Rusty's face. "Sorry," Rusty said. He bolted out the door and along the boardwalk. At the corner of the Wake-Up Jake he skidded to a halt.

The adjoining building was set back several feet and its roof extended to overhang the plank sidewalk. A tall red-and-white-striped barber pole was tucked in the corner, next to a window. Standing in front of the barber pole were GJ and Gram. They did not look happy. A few feet away, Katie raised her left eyebrow and shook her head. Sheila rolled her eyes. Rusty turned back to his grandparents.

He couldn't blame them for being angry, even if he did have a good reason for disappearing this time. He was trying to think how to explain when, above his head, a wooden sign creaked in the wind. He glanced up. "Fashionable Haircutting," he read aloud. "W.D.

Moses... Wow...That's the famous barber!" Rusty drew a deep breath and continued on quickly, hoping to divert their attention. "Do you know? Wellington Delaney Moses was a black man who came here from the United States and opened a barbershop. One day James Barry came in for a haircut and Moses recognized the gold stickpin he was wearing because it looked exactly like a man's face."

Gram and GJ did not look impressed, but Rusty pressed on.

"The stickpin belonged to Moses' friend Charles Blessing, and Moses was already worried because his friend went missing on the road from Quesnel. So he turned Barry in, and Barry was tried by Judge Begbie up in Richfield, and they hung him for murdering Blessing and..." His voice trailed off.

"Rusty."

"And Moses was famous for his Hair Invigorator too. It restored hair in one week." He paused, but they only kept looking at him, so he started for the door.

"Russell!" Gram's voice was sharp, no-nonsense. It stopped him in his tracks. Gram was a tall, slender woman with dark, curly hair like Katie's, except that Gram's was mixed with gray. Her green eyes flashed. "Russell J. Gates, you have got to stay with us and not go wandering off on your own without saying a word to anyone.

Believe it or not, your parents expect us to bring all three of you children home to Victoria safe and sound. They do *not* want us to lose you somewhere in the wilds of British Columbia."

Rusty's eyes shifted to his grandfather, but there was no hint of sympathy in those blue eyes. Grampa Jerry was a few inches taller than Gram, a stocky man whose hair, what there was left of it, was a pale imitation of the fiery red it had once been. "Your grandmother is right, Russell. If you can't stay with the group, we'll have to make other arrangements."

Rusty gulped. "Sorry, it won't happen again." He almost added, *I promise*, but changed his mind, just to be on the safe side, because it's never a good plan to make a promise you're not sure you can keep. He wondered what *arrangements* GJ had in mind.

The important thing now was to change the subject. "Let's go inside. I want to see that Hair Invigorator Moses invented. Hey, GJ! Maybe you could buy some and rub it all over your head before it's too late!"

Gram tried not to laugh, but couldn't help herself. Her face crinkled up. "I wonder if it works," she said.

Katie and Sheila had already disappeared inside the shop, so Rusty barged in after them. He almost crashed into Katie just inside the door. She held up one hand and pointed at the floor with the other.

On the otherwise clean plank floor was the faint outline of a dusty bootprint. A bootprint with a most unusual tread. Before Rusty could look more closely, Gram and GJ crowded into the shop behind him.

"Oh, look!" Katie stepped around the print to grab GJ by the arm. She pointed at a shelf. "There's the famous Hair Invigorator. Let's go see." While Katie and Sheila diverted his grandparents, Rusty glanced around to be sure no one was looking, then pulled the rubbing from his sketchbook and placed it beside the dusty print on the floor.

An exact match!

He scooped up the paper and nodded at Katie, whose brown eyes peeked over Gram's shoulder. Tucking the paper back into his sketchbook, Rusty joined the group.

Several bottles of Hair Invigorator were crowded together on a narrow shelf. Two of them were set apart, and while the others appeared to be empty, these two were full of liquid. They also seemed older somehow, or not so clean.

"Amazing stuff!" Gram said. "It not only restores your hair and revitalizes your skin, but it relieves headaches at the same time." She glanced at Rusty. "I could use some of that right about now."

"What's going on here?" said a sharp voice.

6

Two Dusty Bottles

The middle-aged woman behind them had a thin face, a sharp pointed nose and narrow gray eyes. Her gaze was fixed firmly upon the bottles. She wore a long gingham dress with a wide skirt that skimmed the tops of her button-up boots. Nestled in her frizzy brown hair was a tiny, squashed-looking hat. The overall effect of hair and hat reminded Rusty of bright red feathers from a dead bird caught in a tangled nest. And the way her hair floated around her head like soft brown cotton candy made him wonder if she had rubbed W.D. Moses' Hair Invigorator on her head once too often.

The thin birdlike woman pushed her way through the little group as if she didn't see them standing there. She reached up, took a bottle of Hair Invigorator from the shelf and examined it closely, turning it in her hands. "Dust," she muttered and reached for a second bottle, "sticky, dried-on dust."

"So?" Katie asked. "Aren't they old bottles?"

The woman's narrow eyes flicked to Katie. "I dusted them yesterday just before closing. But there were only three bottles then, I'm certain of it." She frowned and shook her head. "Something weird is going on here—it's almost as if..." Her breath caught and she stared open-mouthed at the bottles in her hands.

"As if what?" Katie prompted.

But the woman turned away. "Nothing at all. I should not have said a thing." She sniffed. "None of the young folk believe in him anyway." Clutching the two dusty bottles close against her stomach, she started out the door.

Rusty ran after her. "Believe in who?" he called, but the woman only walked faster. He followed her out the door. "The ghost of James Evans? I saw him last night!"

Frizzy Hair whirled around. "You?" she glanced quickly from side to side, took two quick steps toward Rusty and glared at him. "What on earth are you talking about, boy?"

Pale gray and intense, her eyes bored into Rusty's. For such a small woman, she had a fierce and terrifying look about her. "Don't you go spreading any rumors," she warned.

Rusty gulped.

"Rusty! Don't you go wandering off again."

He stepped back, relieved to hear his grandmother's voice behind him. "I wasn't going to," he said.

Frizzy Hair swung around and bustled along the plank sidewalk, her wide skirt swinging from side to side like a ringing church bell, her shoulders stooped forward to guard the two dusty bottles in her arms.

A shiny red stagecoach rumbled past on the road below. Fancy lettering on its side shone brilliant yellow, like its tall spoked wheels. Pulled by two patient brown horses, it was packed with tourists.

"Can we go for a stagecoach ride?" Sheila asked.

"I want to see the schoolhouse first," Katie said.

"Let's go to the blacksmith shop," Rusty suggested. Across the street a crowd spilled out through the wide open door of Cameron and Ames Blacksmith Shop, along with the sharp ring of metal hitting metal and the dry, nostril-burning smell of red-hot iron. "There's a demonstration going on over there."

"Hold on, you three," Gram said. "We need to get organized here. We'll have plenty of time to see everything over the next few days, but right now GJ and I will find out about the stagecoach ride. That's a good way to take a quick tour and decide what we want to see first." She consulted her tourist map. "We need to go back to the Visitors' Center to buy tickets. So you three head on over to the blacksmith shop and we'll meet you there."

GJ placed a heavy hand on Rusty's shoulder. "Listen, it's important that you three stick close together and no one wanders off alone. Sheila, since you're the oldest..."

"She's the same age as me!" Katie protested.

"I'm twelve," Sheila reminded her. "Exactly how old are you?"

Katie pulled a face at her best friend. Sheila had turned twelve in June, but Katie's birthday was still two weeks away.

"And you have more sense than these two put together," GJ continued. "I'm counting on you to see that my grandchildren don't do anything stupid."

Sheila gulped. "I'll do my best, GJ," she promised, "but it won't be easy."

GJ threw back his head and laughed. "Don't I know it!" Then he turned serious. "Just stay together. That goes for the entire time we're here, not only this morning. You break that rule and we won't be able to let you out of our sight from then on. Agreed?"

After each of them solemnly promised to keep this rule, Gram and GJ left and Rusty finally had his chance to tell the girls what he overheard at Wake-Up Jake's. Carefully editing out any mention of scalded pants or crunched toes, he told them what the security guards said about the stolen gold. "And I saw him!" he added.

Katie wrinkled her brow. Sheila looked blank.

"The ghost from last night! He went into the Wake-Up Jake."

"He's not a ghost," Katie reminded him. "Haven't you figured that out yet? There's no such thing as ghosts."

"You're sure it was him?" Sheila asked. "All the men who work here wear clothes like that. And most of them have beards too."

"Yeah, but they're all way younger than him. And that footprint in the barbershop? It exactly matches the print we saw last night."

"So I guess that proves he's real," Katie said. "Whoever heard of a ghost that leaves footprints or, for that matter, goes to restaurants? Why should he need to eat if he doesn't have a real body?"

While Rusty thought this over, Katie's eyes slid across the street. "Let's go see if he's still there."

"No!" Rusty absolutely could not go back. What if that man was still there? That huge angry security guard with scalded pants? And then there was the waitress. "I want to see the blacksmith shop."

"You can see that any time. We need to check out your Prospector Man before he leaves." Katie set off across the street without looking back.

"But..." Sheila's eyes darted from one cousin to the other, "we have to stick together," she pleaded. "We promised."

"Then come with me," Katie called over her shoulder. Almost halfway across the dusty road, she stopped to let a stagecoach rumble past.

"Please, Rusty!" Sheila pleaded.

He folded his arms across his chest. "We're supposed to go to the blacksmith shop," he said stubbornly.

"Okay, we'll go there, I promise. Just come across the street with us first. We can't let Katie go wandering off alone. You know what she's like—she'll probably think she's on the trail of some weird mystery, and the next thing we know we'll all be in trouble, just like before."

Rusty hesitated. He didn't want to follow his cousin, but he hated to see Sheila so upset. And he knew she was right. There was no telling what trouble Katie might stir up if left to her own devices. She was already on the steps in front of the Wake-Up Jake...and they did promise GJ.

"Please, Rusty? You don't have to come inside if you don't want. Just walk across the street with me?"

"Oh, all right," he grumbled.

Outside the Wake-Up Jake, Rusty sank onto a bench, stared at the boardwalk in front of his sneakers and tried to imagine he was totally and completely invisible. Sheila hesitated in front of the open door, took a quick breath and stepped inside.

Ten seconds later the white-bearded man stepped out. He paused, plopped his hat over his thick gray hair and turned away from Rusty toward the barbershop next door.

Katie darted out and followed. Two steps behind her, Sheila glanced at Rusty, made a face, jerked her head toward Katie and took off after her friend. Rusty eased to his feet and trailed behind.

He caught up with the girls at the barber pole. "Okay," Sheila was saying, "we came with you. Now you have to go with us to the blacksmith shop."

"But he's in there." Katie nodded toward the barbershop. She pressed her face against the window. "And he's looking at the Hair Invigorator!"

"So what? He's a tourist. Looking at stuff is what tourists do. Katie, he's just a man dressed as a prospector which, believe it or not, is not a crime."

"C'mon, Katie," Rusty said. "Gram and GJ will be back soon and we're supposed to be over at the blacksmith shop."

Katie's dark eyes narrowed. She squinted from Sheila to Rusty to the open shop door, but when Sheila and Rusty started down the stairs from the boardwalk, she followed. "He's up to something, I just know it," she whispered.

"Like what?" Sheila asked.

"I don't know, but I have this *feeling*."

"Right. Katie Reid, Private Investigator—with Feelings."

Katie didn't seem to hear. "Something weird is happening and it has to do with those dusty bottles of Hair Invigorator."

"Yeah," Rusty agreed, "Frizzy Hair sure freaked out about them."

"Hey!" Katie said. "What if your ghost put them there last night?"

Sheila rolled her eyes. "I can't believe this. It's two stupid bottles of Hair Invigorator, guys, simple as that."

"And a bootprint," Rusty reminded her.

"Exactly," Katie said. "So tonight we keep watch until midnight."

Rusty could not believe how uncomfortable the stagecoach ride was. Even on this relatively smooth dirt road, every bump sent a shudder from the narrow spoke wheels up through the coach, over the impossibly hard wooden seat and into his backside. By the end of a half hour he could hardly wait to get out. He could not imagine spending long hours, day after day, riding over rugged mountain trails on the narrow, rutted Cariboo Wagon Road in a contraption like this, just to reach Barkerville. People must have had tougher butts in those days, he decided and was wondering if they developed calluses when Gram touched his shoulder.

"If we hurry," she said, "we can catch the mining demonstration down behind town by Williams Creek."

Rows of benches were set out in front of a tall Cornish waterwheel. A long flume, or wooden trough, ran high above their heads. Supported by tall posts, the flume diverted water from Williams Creek, which was higher up, to spill out directly above the waterwheel.

Two young men wearing white shirts open at the neck, vests, long pants, tall leather boots and the inevitable hats stood beside the wheel, chatting quietly. One had a short thick beard, so dark it appeared almost black. The other had wide, light brown sideburns and a huge handlebar mustache that made Rusty think of a walrus.

The mustached one walked over to stand in front of the benches, crowded with tourists. "Ladies and gentlemen," he began, "welcome to Barkerville, the largest community west of Toronto and north of San Francisco. Whether you made the long trek here by foot, on horseback or traveling by Barnard's Express, I fear you are bound for bitter disappointment. Thousands have arrived before you only to realize the sad but unavoidable truth. Since the day 'Dutch' Bill Dietz first struck gold on Williams Creek up at Richfield, things have changed drastically. In this year of 1870, you can no longer stake out a claim on the creek and pan for your fortune in gold. Any gold that remains now lies buried deep beneath the gravel, below the blue clay, on bedrock. To reach it requires the digging of shafts deep underground, which means investing a great deal of money in equipment, such as this Cornish waterwheel and flume you see before you."

Rusty couldn't take his eyes off the man's mustache. Perched firmly on his upper lip, it wriggled sinuously up and down, forward and back, like a small animal as he talked. Rusty nudged Katie to see if she noticed.

He hardly recognized his cousin. She had the sappiest expression on her face that he had ever seen. Her eyes remained on Mustache Man as she reached over to touch Sheila's arm. This was too weird. Sheila had an identical expression on her face. "He's so cute!" Katie whispered.

Sheila sighed.

Rusty gagged.

He glanced around to see if anyone else was mesmerized by Mustache Man. That's when he noticed someone seated at the far end of the very last bench. Red-and-black-checked shirt, vest, hat and dark sunglasses over a full white beard. In the harsh light of day, Rusty could not believe this was the ghost of Three Finger Evans. What did Katie call him? Prospector Man. Rusty nudged his cousin again. "He's here."

"Who cares?" Katie sighed.

"But...you're the one who wanted to follow him."

Katie turned slowly toward Rusty. Gradually her eyes cleared. She frowned. "What?"

"Prospector Man, from Wake-Up Jake's. I thought you wanted to follow him. Don't look, but he's behind us at the end of the back bench."

Katie's head swiveled around and jerked back again. "He's watching us!" she whispered.

"I told you not to look."

"Sh!" Gram said from the bench directly behind.

Rusty tried to concentrate as the two men explained how it all worked. The flume carried water from the creek, which fell on the wheel and made it go around, which made the pump work, which carried gravel and water out of the shaft to be placed in a sluice that would capture gold particles while water and lighter gravel flowed back to the creek.

So who was that man at the back? Why was he dressed as a prospector if he didn't work here? Was it him they saw last night and not Three Finger's ghost at all? Rusty glanced over his shoulder. Prospector Man slipped his sunglasses down and peered over them. Slate gray eyes, cold as steel, bored into Rusty's face.

Rusty gulped. Something weird was going on, and he needed time to sort it out.

Earlier, at the restaurant, the waitress had said, *Nice work!* But did she mean his sketch, which she had obviously looked at because his book was closed when he left it there, or was she commenting on the way he spilled coffee on the big guard's pants? Rusty had no idea, so he switched to something else that needed thinking about.

Where did those two dusty old bottles of Hair Invigorator come from? What did Frizzy Hair know about it? Could the bottles have been put there by the ghost of Three Finger Evans? And if so, why?

"Aren't you coming, Rusty?" Katie called.

"Give your head a shake, boy," GJ whispered and nudged him from behind.

Rusty hurried over to the waterwheel. Mustache Man, Dark Beard, Katie, Sheila and a small woman were already there. The woman was older than Gram and wore sneakers, jeans, a long-sleeved shirt, a straw hat with a blue ribbon and oval sunglasses.

Dark Beard picked up a pan that looked like a large pie plate and was filled with water and gravel. "The idea is that gold is heavy," he explained as he sloshed the water around in the pan. "So it sinks to the bottom while sand and water and gravel spill out. Watch how I do it, then each of you can have a turn."

Slowly he rotated the pan. The woman stepped closer to Rusty. "It feels so strange to be here after 136 years," she murmured, seemingly to herself.

Rusty's jaw dropped. He tried not to stare, but couldn't help himself. Obviously she had left a part of her brain somewhere along the road to Barkerville. The woman was old all right, but sure as anything she was nowhere near 136 years old!

"Now it's your turn," Dark Beard said. "Who's first?"

Rusty dragged his eyes away from the 136-year-old woman. "Me!" he said and reached out with both hands to take the large metal pan. His arms drooped. It was heavier than he expected. Dark Beard showed him how to tip the pan slightly and rotate it in a smooth motion, allowing water and gravel to slosh over its rim. When most of the water and gravel were gone, Rusty looked at what remained. His eyes widened. Like little kernels of popcorn that hadn't popped, a cluster of gold particles had worked their way to the bottom of the pan. "I'm rich!" he shouted.

"Not quite," Dark Beard told him, snatching the gold pan away. "We mix gold nuggets with the gravel so tourists can see how it works. Besides, any gold you find here belongs to Barkerville Historic Town."

As Dark Beard refilled the gold pan, Rusty had the feeling that other eyes were watching him. He glanced over his shoulder. Prospector Man was looking directly at him, his eyes impossible to see behind dark sunglasses.

7

Prospector Man

By mid-afternoon everyone had done enough sight-seeing for one day, so they climbed wearily onto their bikes and rode back to the campground. After a cold drink and a large snack, Rusty and the girls were full of energy again and decided to take a bike ride around the campground.

"Be sure to be back in an hour," GJ told them. "We're going to drive up to Bowron Lake and have a swim before dinner."

The campsites were large and quite private, set back in the trees on both sides of two parallel roads. The roads were joined at each end by a semicircular drive and so formed a long, narrow oval. A short road cut through the center of the oval, running from the campground entrance through to the back road.

Turning left out of their campsite, they rode to the far end of the front road and around the curve to the back one. A campsite on their right had two small yellow tents in it, shaped like igloos. Rusty glanced at a white van as they passed the next campsite to the left. Suddenly Katie screeched to a halt in front of him, leapt off her bike as if she'd been stung, pulled the bike onto the grass beside the road, dropped it and slunk toward the bushes. Rusty stopped to watch.

Farther down the road, Sheila also stopped. She looked back in time to see Katie crouch down and part the low tree branches in front of her. Sheila shook her head sadly and stayed where she was.

Rusty couldn't stand it. He had to know what Katie was looking at. So he dropped his bike near Katie's and crept up behind her. Through a gap in the trees they could see right back to the campsite they had just passed. A shiny white camper van was backed in close to the picnic table where a man was seated. He wore a red checked shirt and brown vest. Wispy strands of white hair snaked out from under his wide-brimmed hat and curled over his ears. A full white beard flowed over his chest, and little square glasses perched on the tip of his nose as he studied a large sheet of paper on the table in front of him. He ran one beefy finger in a wiggly line over the paper.

Prospector Man. Or was he? Rusty spent so much time sketching that he had learned to notice small details most people missed. He realized now that although the man's clothes and beard were the same, something had changed—something in the set of his shoulders, the way they slumped so low over the table. However, he reasoned, that could be due to the way he was sitting, leaning over to study the paper. Or it could be because he was tired. Hadn't the man spent half the night wandering around the campground and most of the day touring Barkerville? That was enough to make anyone's shoulders slump.

The man reached for a bottle of beer on the far corner of his paper. A large ashtray with the stem of a pipe poking out held down the opposite corner. When he picked up his beer, the paper flapped in the wind and he slapped his hand on it. Suddenly his head jerked up and he peered over his glasses at the exact spot where they were hiding.

The man plunked the bottle down and leaned forward to push himself heavily from the picnic table. Giving a loud, wheezy cough, he hitched up his pants and swung one short chunky leg over the bench. Before he moved his other leg, they were gone.

Katie reached her bike first. She pushed it onto the road, wheeled it around in the direction they had come from and hopped on. Rusty followed reluctantly and Sheila swung her bike around. As they passed the short drive leading into the man's campsite, he had almost reached the road. With a book tucked under one arm, he puffed on his pipe and watched them ride past. Rusty's stomach flipped over. He wished they had taken off in the opposite direction, away from the man.

Moments later, quite suddenly and with a sense of relief, he realized Katie had made the right decision. If they had ridden away from Prospector Man's campsite, the man would know something was wrong because he should have seen them pass by as he walked toward the road. Instead, they rode toward him, as if they had just now arrived from farther down the back road.

Before they rounded the curve, Rusty glanced back and was relieved to see the man headed down the road away from them. They had almost reached the front road when Katie turned her bike around. "Let's go!" she whispered.

"Where?" Sheila asked.

"Back to that campsite, of course. We need to find out what he was looking at."

Sheila shook her head. "No!"

But Katie was already out of sight around the curve. Rusty and Sheila caught up as Katie leaped off her bike just short of the campsite.

"You can't be serious," Sheila whispered. "He could come back at any minute."

"He won't," Katie said confidently. "He's gone down to the washroom and he took a book with him. Don't you know? Men that age sit there, like, forever. So we have plenty of time to take a look."

"But why should we want to?"

"Because if he's the same man who went creeping past our campsite last night, I want to find out what he's up to."

"Why?" Sheila demanded.

"Remember what Rusty overheard in the Wake-Up Jake? People who read *Spirits of the Cariboo* will soon be rushing up here to search for Three Finger's gold. I think the rush has already started, and unless I miss my guess, this guy has a map that can help find it."

Much as Rusty hated to admit it, this made sense to him. "I'll come with you," he offered.

"I'll wait here," Sheila said. "If I see him coming I'll whistle like this." She placed two fingers against her lips and gave a loud, shrill whistle.

Katie and Rusty left their bikes at the roadside and ran into the campsite. They stopped at the picnic table and studied the paper.

"It's a map of Barkerville," Katie said.

Rusty nodded. "But not just Barkerville—all the trails and old mines and cabins in the whole area."

"Wow! I wonder where he got it."

Rusty studied the legend in the bottom right-hand corner. "I don't know, but it looks just like one my dad gave me, which is a copy of an old map from before the fire in 1868." Rusty rubbed the curled corner of the map between his fingertips. It felt thin and crisp and was yellowed with age.

A short ruler lay at an angle across the map, marking a route between Barkerville and a miner's cabin up to the west, near Lowhee Creek.

"Do you think—" Katie stopped abruptly. She listened for a second then whispered, "Did you hear that?"

"What?" Then Rusty heard it too. A loud snort. *Bear!* he thought, and his heart stopped beating.

There it was again! Not a snort but a sneeze. And it came from inside the camper van behind them. The springs creaked. The van wobbled.

"Let's go!" Katie whispered.

They started for the road. A shrill whistle stopped them dead. Swinging around, they ran for the trees behind the campsite. As they passed the van, Rusty saw a small red motorcycle propped against its back bumper. They crashed through trees and bushes, heading for the next campsite. At first Rusty thought it was empty, but as they skirted around a thick fir tree, he noticed a small tent-trailer. They stopped again, undecided.

Rrrr-whump. A van door slid open behind them.

They ran into the tent-trailer's campsite, skirted behind the trailer, reached the front road and ran around the curve. Rusty was sure that their two bikes, lying on the roadside near the campsite, would give them away. But his fears vanished when, before reaching the back road, they saw Sheila standing close against some bushes where she had moved all three bikes.

"I don't think that man saw you in his campsite," she whispered, "because he was still a long way down the road when I whistled."

While they paused to catch their breath, Katie told Sheila about the map and the sneeze. They climbed on their bikes, continued on to the back road and cycled past Prospector Man's campsite as fast as they could pedal. Rusty was afraid to look. He followed the girls to the far end of the campground.

In the lead as usual, Sheila stopped at the bottom of a dirt trail that wound invitingly into the forest. A wooden sign pointing up the trail identified it as the *Lowhee Walking Trail.*

"Want to go up there?" Sheila asked eagerly.

"Not today," Katie said. "We're going swimming, remember?"

Rusty jumped off his bike and leaned it against the trailer before he realized that three people were seated on folding chairs in the shade of the awning. Gram, GJ and an older woman with black and gray-streaked hair and light blue eyes. She looked vaguely familiar as she dabbed at her damp forehead with a clean, white handkerchief. The three adults were chatting, sipping tall glasses of iced tea and swatting flies with their hats.

"Hey! Here they are," GJ said. "Joyce, I'd like you to meet our two grandchildren, Katie Reid and Russell Gates, and our friend, Sheila Walton. Kids, this is Joyce Evans—but I guess you already met her at the gold-mining demo. Gram and I got to chatting with her and asked her to stop by this afternoon."

"Ms. Evans came all the way from Cornwall, Ontario, to visit Barkerville," Gram added.

Rusty recognized her now, the 136-year-old woman. She looked different without her hat and sunglasses.

"Then," Katie said, "you must be from that white camper van we saw."

Joyce Evans frowned. "Why do you say that?"

"Because it has Ontario license plates."

"Well, you're very observant, Katie, but actually I drove here in my Jeep, towing my little tent-trailer."

"We were telling Ms. Evans about your interest in history, Rusty," Gram said. "She would like to borrow that book your dad gave you because she hadn't heard about it before leaving home and may want to buy a copy."

"Listen," Ms. Evans stood up, "thank you so much for the tea, but I know you folks are anxious to go swimming, so I'll be off now. Perhaps tomorrow afternoon the five of you will come down to my campsite for refreshments? And Rusty, maybe you could bring the book along then?"

"We'd love to," Gram said. "Around 4:00?"

"Perfect." Ms. Evans started to walk away, then stopped and turned back. "By the way, did any of you happen to come across an old map of Barkerville today? Perhaps folded up and left on a bench near the Cornish wheel?"

They shook their heads.

Ms. Evans pressed her hand to her forehead as if it hurt. "I must be getting forgetful. I know I brought it with me, but I seem to have misplaced it since arriving here."

"Oh?" GJ asked. "That's too bad, but you should be able to get another one easily enough."

"The thing of it is, this particular map belonged to my late husband's family. It's really very old."

8

The Map

They swam out from the shoreline of shallow, muddy Bowron Lake. Out here, so long as they whispered, no one could overhear.

"I told you that man was up to something," Katie said.

"You mean Prospector Man?" Rusty asked.

Sheila rolled over and floated on her back, gazing up at the clear blue sky. "What are you talking about?"

"It's obvious," Katie said. "He stole Ms. Evans' map."

"You don't know that. Just because he has an old map doesn't mean he *stole* it. And besides, doesn't Rusty have one just like it? Maybe Rusty is the one who stole Ms. Evans' map."

"Don't be so dumb, Sheila. You know my dad gave me those maps, and he copied them at the archives." Rusty tried to tread water without straightening out his legs because he really didn't want his toes to touch the mucky lake bottom. He bent his knees, cupped his hands and did a vigorous dog paddle to keep his head above water. "But anyway..." Water splashed into his eyes and mouth and he tried to paddle a little less energetically. "Anyway, don't you think it's a huge coincidence?"

Katie narrowed her eyes. "If you mean that Ms. Evans lost an old map and Prospector Man had one on his picnic table, then yes, because that map was ancient."

Rusty nodded. "But that's not what I meant." When his chin sank underwater he straightened his knees just a little, just enough that he could kick gently to keep himself afloat. His big toe dipped into something slimy. "Ugh!" He curled his legs up again.

"So what's a coincidence then?" Katie asked.

"Her name! I mean, think about it, Joyce Evans—Three Finger Evans—they've got to be related."

"No way," Sheila said. "There must be a jillion people named Evans in Canada."

"But," Rusty insisted, "she comes from Cornwall."

"So?"

"So Three Finger Evans came from Cornwall, Ontario. Didn't you read the book?"

"Nope," Sheila curled forward and did a lazy somersault in the water.

"Ms. Evans said the map belonged to her husband's family," Katie said and promptly disappeared below the surface. She popped back up, sputtering and coughing. "But guess what. So does Prospector Man!"

Nothing showed of Sheila except the top of her head, her eyes and her nose, but she managed to look totally confused. She floated up high enough to ask, "Prospector Man belongs to Ms. Evans' husband's family?"

"Huh?" Katie wrinkled her forehead. "No! I mean he comes from Cornwall too. There's a decal with the name of his car dealership on the back of his van and it's in Cornwall, Ontario."

"Now *that* is a coincidence," Sheila agreed. She kicked her legs and swam away with strong, steady strokes.

Rusty watched her go, knowing he could never hope to keep up with her. Neither could Katie, but she would never admit it. His eyes rolled toward his cousin. She was floating on her back with ten toes sticking out of the water.

"She doesn't want to get involved," Katie whispered.

"I know."

"Because she promised her mom."

"Yeah." Rusty hesitated, then added, "I kind of did too."

"What?"

"I promised not to cause any trouble for Gram and GJ."

"Oh, that. Well, so did I, but only because Mom and Dad forced me. Anyhow, the way I figure it is, if Gram and GJ don't know, then it won't cause them any trouble. Right?"

"I guess." Rusty wasn't quite sure this was what his parents had in mind—but hey! Whatever worked.

"And anyway," Katie added, "it's not as if there are a bunch of bad guys involved up here, not like before. It's only some people who want to get rich quick."

"So you think Prospector Man is after the gold?"

"Looks that way."

"And Ms. Evans too?"

"Could be." Katie curled into a ball, floating with only her face above the surface. "And don't forget about those two security guards you overheard. And Frizzy Hair. She's up to something, unless I miss my guess. We need to outsmart them all and find the gold ourselves. Then everyone will have to take us seriously from now on."

"Maybe," Rusty said doubtfully, "but who knows how many other people are looking for it. Since *Spirits of the Cariboo* hit the bookstores, tons of people could show up here this summer hoping to find that gold. What makes you think we can find it?"

"Simple," Katie said. "Just like any good detectives, we follow the clues. Plus we have all the old maps. And I bet Ms. Evans knows more than she's letting on, so we need to keep a close eye on her."

When they returned to the campground after swimming, Gram and GJ set about barbecuing hamburgers for dinner; Katie settled at the picnic table, bent over her notebook; Sheila sprawled in a folding chair, listening to music; and Rusty spread out his maps next to Katie at the table.

The first map showed the actual townsite of Barkerville, as it looked back in 1870 after being rebuilt following the fire. The second one showed all the claims staked on Williams Creek, from the original town of Richfield to the south, right down Williams Creek to Camerontown on the north side of Barkerville. The third map, the one that really interested him, showed all the old prospectors' trails and roads in the entire area. Except that the paper was new and the printing much clearer, it looked the same as the map they saw on Prospector Man's picnic table. Rusty studied it closely.

Most of the trails that led through the woods and up the mountainsides around Barkerville had little drawings of tiny log cabins scattered here and there along them. Near many of the smaller creeks that flowed into Williams Creek were little squares, and next to many of the squares were spoked wheels.

Rusty checked out the map's legend. Just as he suspected, the log houses showed where miners' cabins had been located, the squares were openings to mine shafts, and the wheels identified Cornish waterwheels. With growing excitement, he opened *Spirits of the Cariboo* and skimmed through the Three Finger Evans story once more.

Beside him, his cousin was still writing like mad in her notebook, which set Rusty to wondering what she could possibly write about for so long. He leaned closer.

"Get away, Rusty!" Katie shrieked and picked up one side of the book to block his view. She glared at him over it, her brown eyes furious.

Okay, now that he had her full attention, he may as well take advantage of it. "Look at this!" he said.

Katie frowned, glanced at the map, back down at her notebook, then over at the map again. She snapped her notebook shut and clutched it in one hand as she slid along the bench to see the map better.

"One of those little cabins must have belonged to Three Finger Evans," Rusty said.

Katie nodded. "But which one?"

"The book says his cabin was northwest of Barkerville toward Lowhee Creek. And look here," he placed a finger on the map, "there's a cabin right there on Lowhee Trail—do you think it's the same trail that starts here at the campground?"

"Could be. There's one way to find out for sure."

They looked at Sheila. She was leaning back on a folding chair under the awning, earphones on, eyes closed, fingers snapping and feet tapping to her favorite music. The two cousins nodded at one another and smiled.

"This is the best hamburger I ever ate in my life," Rusty said, using the back of his hand to wipe away the juices that ran down his chin.

"Yes," Gram agreed, "you look like you're enjoying it."

"Sheila wants to go for a walk up the Lowhee Walking Trail after supper," Katie said. "Don't you, Sheila?"

Next to Katie at the picnic table, Sheila had a mouthful of hamburger. Her blue eyes opened wide with surprise, but all she could do was nod.

"Aren't you kids tired?" GJ asked. "We've had a busy day."

"Nope!" Rusty said. "I can hardly wait to go for a walk. Besides," he patted his stomach, "I need some exercise to work up an appetite for dessert."

GJ shook his head. "I don't know where you get all that energy!"

"We can have dessert when you get back," Gram said, "but don't forget you've got to clean up the dishes before you leave."

When they walked out of their campsite, they turned right and headed along the front road as far as the entrance road. There they turned right again, cut through to the back road and headed for the trail.

"Look!" Rusty whispered to Katie.

Near the bottom of Lowhee Trail, a man moved quickly, his hands jammed into his pockets. He was dressed in period costume, complete with wide-brimmed hat, bandanna, checked shirt, vest and pants tucked into high boots. They caught a glimpse of white beard before he disappeared up the trail.

9

Spy or Be Spied Upon

"Why do I get the feeling this isn't exactly going to be a nature hike?" Sheila said as they started up the trail.

"Are you kidding?" Rusty asked. "Why else would we go traipsing through the woods?"

"We know how much you like nature hikes," Katie added, "so here we are."

Sheila's eyes darted suspiciously from one to the other of the cousins, then were drawn toward the steep, well-groomed trail that lead invitingly into a forest of lodge-pole pine, fir and spruce. "Okay," she said finally, "just be really quiet and we might see some wildlife."

Sheila led the way while Rusty, last in line, concentrated on keeping up with the girls and keeping his mouth shut. He wondered what sort of wildlife they might see. He thought about bears. And he thought about the two chocolate bars he stashed in his backpack before leaving the campsite.

If bears could smell chocolate right through the wrappers, then the best way to get rid of the scent would be to eat the chocolate bars. Problem solved. He stopped and slid his backpack from his shoulders, but then another thought struck him. *Aren't you supposed to make tons of noise if bears are around?*

Hurriedly pulling on his backpack, Rusty started up the trail after the girls, singing loud enough to burst a lung. Even so, he expected at any minute to go winging around a corner and come face to face with a bear. Not just any bear, but a huge, angry mother bear determined to protect her cubs.

He stopped. Listened. Nothing. Where were Katie and Sheila? *But wait, what was that?* His heart thudded into his ribs. He held his breath. *There it was again*! *A footstep?*

Thud.

Yes! Heavy, plodding footsteps. Behind him. Getting closer. A chill shot through him. Certain that a black bear was hot on the scent of his chocolate bars, Rusty took off as fast as he could run up the steep trail. He sped around one bend and then another until, gasping for air, he came to a fork in the trail. He glanced from left to right, danced from one foot to the other. Which way? He could feel that angry bear closing in on him, almost smell its powerful odor.

Sheila would know what to do. She and her mom went backpacking in the mountains all the time. He had to find the girls. But left or right? Right or left? Why did they take off without him? Was it a trick? Were they trying to get rid of him once and for all? Feed him to a hungry mother bear?

Then he noticed it. Impaled on a bush by the right-hand trail was a sheet of lined paper, just like the ones in Katie's notebook. He ripped it from the bush. Printed in pencil were the initials "K" and "S", with an arrow pointing up the trail. Rusty scrunched up the paper, glanced back and took off. Up and up he ran, but the trail seemed to get steeper with every stride until, legs aching, lungs straining, he hobbled around a corner and there they were.

"Rusty!" Katie said. "What happened to you? We were starting back to look for you."

Rusty opened his mouth to say, *A bear!* But he was so short of breath, all that came out was, "A b...!"

"A buh?" Sheila asked, frowning.

Rusty gulped air through his mouth but could not draw enough oxygen into his lungs. A pulse beat loud and hard in his ears. Feeling dizzy, he bent forward, hands on knees. Sheila took several steps down the trail until she could see around the bend. She stopped, listened and ran back. "Quick!" she whispered. "Into the bushes!"

It seemed to Rusty that hiding in the bushes might not be the best plan with a hungry bear on their trail, but he had no energy to object. He followed the girls through the undergrowth toward a big fir tree. Sheila reached the fir, squeezed behind it and peered out the other side. "Get down!"

Katie and Rusty ducked.

Enveloped in thick bush, Rusty listened for the deep *woof, woof, woof* of a black bear's breathing. Instead he heard footsteps. They came closer and closer up the trail until they were opposite his hiding place. They stopped. Rusty squeezed his eyes shut. He would have held his breath, but his lungs cried so desperately for oxygen that he concentrated instead on breathing as softly as possible. Any second now the powerful animal would charge into the bushes, growling, swiping those giant paws, those long, sharp claws at anything that breathed. "Oh please, oh please, oh please!" he whispered. "Please don't let me get eaten!"

The bushes behind him rustled. A heavy paw landed on his shoulder. "WHA." Rusty leaped to his feet, ready to run screaming through the bushes, to climb the nearest tree, to...

"It's okay now," Katie said. "He's gone."

"The bear?"

Katie's forehead crinkled, her left eyebrow rose. "What bear? I'm talking about the man who walked past us. Come on, we need to follow him before he gets away!"

Rusty followed his cousin through the bushes back to the trail. Sheila was already there, pacing back and forth, fists clenched, bristling with anger. "You knew about this, didn't you? Both of you!" Beneath her freckles, Sheila's face flushed pink. Her bright blue eyes flashed from Rusty to Katie. "I knew I couldn't trust you two! *Why else would we go traipsing through the woods?* Oh, sure, Rusty! *We know how much you like nature hikes!* Right, Katie!"

Sheila raised her fists, pressed them against her cheeks. "I don't know how, but you two knew that man was coming up here and you wanted to follow him!" She dropped her hands. "So you pretended to be nice! You pretended to do something I like for a change! How could I be so stupid?"

Rusty studied the toes of his sneakers. Did they really do that? Did they *pretend* to be nice? And what did she mean, *something I like for a change*? He was the one who felt left out, not Sheila.

"You're wrong, Sheila," Katie told her. "We wanted to explore the trail. We had no idea about that man coming up here—we don't even know who he is, do we, Rusty?"

Rusty shook his head. Sheila glared straight through him. He looked down at his sneakers again and thought about the maps stashed in his backpack along with the chocolate bars. "Okay, I admit, *maybe* we wanted to check out other stuff besides wildlife, but we didn't know anyone else would be up here. How could we?"

"Except for that man we saw at the start of the trail," Katie added.

There was a long silence while everyone glared at everyone else. Finally Sheila's shoulders slumped and she said, "Sorry, guys. It's just..." She drew a deep breath. "Sometimes I feel, you know, kind of left out? Because you guys are all family and I'm, well, I'm not. And..." she bit her lip, "the worst thing is, my own mother doesn't even want me around!"

"It's for your own good," Rusty reminded her and suddenly felt like his father. "Because she's busy working all summer."

"And because she thought you'd have fun with us," Katie said. "I thought you were having fun."

"I am." Sheila sighed. "But don't you ever get homesick?"

Katie and Rusty shook their heads. "We go on vacation with Gram and GJ every summer," Katie explained. "Usually it's just for a couple of weeks though."

"Okay. Maybe that's why I feel left out. I keep thinking Rusty doesn't want me here."

"Me? Ha!" Rusty said. "Are you kidding? You think I want to be left alone with Katie? Can you imagine what sort of trouble she'd get me into?"

For a moment Katie looked angry, but when Sheila burst out laughing, they all did, breaking the tension. Then Katie asked, "But why did you think we knew about that man? Who is he? I didn't even see him."

"It was that old prospector guy with the white beard."

"Prospector Man?" Rusty said. "That's impossible. We saw him go up the trail ahead of us. Hey! He must have hid in the bushes, just like we did, and watched us go by. He's following us!"

"If he is," Sheila pointed out, "he isn't doing a very good job."

"One thing's for sure," Katie said, "if we waste any more time we'll never catch up to him, and we really need to find out what he's up to, so let's go!"

Rusty and Sheila watched Katie's swiftly retreating back. Her bright red T-shirt was the last thing to disappear through the trees.

Rusty knew Sheila was still unhappy, in spite of what she said, but he could not believe that Sheila, of all people, felt left out. Why should she? If anyone felt left out, it should be him. And he did sometimes. He liked Sheila. Really. But she was Katie's friend, not his. So what was he supposed to do now? How could he make her feel welcome?

"Please, Sheila, come with us? I'm really gonna need

your help with Katie." Okay, maybe that didn't quite do the trick. "I mean—I really like you, Sheila."

Oh, man! That didn't sound right either. Rusty felt his face turn bright red. Sheila gave him an odd look, as if she weren't quite sure what to think.

"That is...I mean..." Rusty stammered.

To his relief, Sheila grinned and lightly punched his shoulder. "Don't worry, Rusty, I know what you're trying to say. Come on, we'd better catch up with Katie."

Around every bend, Rusty expected to see Katie just ahead of them, but the path continued on and on forever, climbing, turning, twisting this way and that, until he was once again struggling to pull enough oxygen into his lungs.

Where was Katie? *Puff...puff...gasp...*How did she get so far ahead? *Gasp... puff...puff...*His feet felt heavy, his legs ached. "Sheila!" he breathed. "I need a rest!" But she didn't hear him.

Rusty dragged himself around the next bend and saw Sheila, her back to him, head twisted to one side.

"What?" he whispered.

"I heard something."

He listened. What he heard was the sound of air wheezing into his lungs. If Sheila heard something else, he really didn't care right now. He was happy enough simply to stand still.

Sheila charged into the bushes.

Rusty groaned and followed her up a steep, almost over-grown path that was rocky underfoot and slippery with moss kept damp by a trickle of water that snaked around the rocks. All he could see of Sheila was a patch of blue T-shirt through the foliage. She stopped again. "Listen!"

Rusty heard a faint sound, but whether it was a human voice or the whisper of water or even the sigh of wind in the trees above his head, he could not determine. Then Sheila pointed at something ahead of them, almost hid-den in the trees. A patch of red. A T-shirt. Katie.

Crouched low, she motioned at them, but when they came up beside her, Katie's eyes were fixed on some-thing farther ahead. About ten meters away, partially hid-den by thick undergrowth, a figure stood absolutely still. Although he had not seen the man who passed them on the trail, Rusty knew instantly this was him. He was dressed in prospector's clothing, complete with red-and-black-checked shirt, but his head was bare. His back to them, he held his wide-brimmed hat at his side.

Prospector Man faced the trunk of a tree that divid-ed in two to form a convenient V just above shoulder height. He peered through this opening at something in front of him.

The crack of a stick breaking underfoot was followed by a rustling sound, as if a large animal was moving through the bushes beyond Prospector Man. Rusty's eyes followed the sound until he caught a brief glimpse of a white beard and a wide-brimmed hat. What? Another Prospector Man? What was going on?

This second man moved back and forth as if searching for something. Rusty pictured the map in his backpack, the one that showed an old miner's cabin up this way, the same map they saw in Prospector Man's campsite. Was Prospector Man hoping to find the cabin, just like he and Katie were? And who was the second bearded prospector?

Rusty gasped. It had to be Three Finger Evans, still searching for his old cabin and his fortune in gold.

A sudden movement caught Rusty's attention. Prospector Man's hand jerked up to his face. His entire body convulsed. He sneezed. Not loud, but enough. Everything stopped. Everyone held their breath.

Three Finger's ghost took off like a shot into the bushes, away from the sneeze. Rusty expected Prospector Man to chase after him, but instead, to his horror, the man pushed away from the tree trunk and swung around.

He came barreling through the forest directly toward them.

10

Three Whiskey Bottles

They ran.

"Hey!" Prospector Man yelled. "Hey, you! Stop right there!"

The steep, rough terrain and slippery rocks underfoot slowed them down. Behind Katie, Rusty forced himself to concentrate as he had never concentrated in his life before. He must not slip. If he fell here...

Concentrate. He kept his eyes on Katie's new white sneakers, watched them bounce from side to side over the slippery rocks. He stepped in the exact same spots and held his arms out from his sides, brushing the tops of overhanging bushes. If he slipped he would grab on and prevent himself from falling. Falling...tumbling feet first into a deep, dark tunnel. Cold and slimy. Unable to get out.

Rusty shook his head. *Concentrate.* But he had lost precious seconds and now could no longer see Katie.

"Get back here, you interfering little brats!" Prospector Man was so close, Rusty felt the ground tremble. The toe of a heavy boot crashed down solidly on his heel.

"AAARGH!" It hurt so bad it brought tears to his eyes. Ignoring the pain, Rusty kept going. He stumbled. Something was wrong with his foot. *Oh, man!* His sneaker had slipped off his heel! He staggered around a sharp bend and caught a glimpse of red, low down, ahead and to his left; of blue to his right. He saw a thin straight branch lying across the trail. In that instant he knew. He had to reach that branch, cross over it and get out of the way. Fast.

Almost there—right above it—footsteps at his heels. He threw himself forward, crashed against the ground and skidded. His elbows scraped over loose rocks, hurting, but he scrambled to his hands and knees and kept moving.

"AIHHH!" Prospector Man's angry yell filled the forest. It was followed by an ominous roar, like the rumble of an avalanche. Rocks clattered, and a string of swear words rose to the treetops.

Katie and Sheila yanked Rusty to his feet. They ran.

"Quick," Sheila said when they reached the trail, "fix your shoe!"

He bent down, yanked open the Velcro, slid his foot in properly, slapped the Velcro in place and ran, scarcely aware that his heel hurt with every step.

They ran down and down until they reached the back road of the campground, where they stopped to catch their breath. Katie's face was the color of a ripe tomato and, except for her brown freckles, Sheila's was bright pink. "Let's get out of here," she said.

"Prospector Man is gonna be mad!" Katie warned.

Rusty grinned. "The man should learn to watch where he's going."

"What happened to you three?" Gram asked when they walked into their campsite. She and GJ were seated at the picnic table, across from one another, playing a game of cribbage.

"What do you mean?" Katie asked.

"Your faces are bright pink, you're out of breath and you look as if you'd just completed a marathon." Gram moved a peg forward on the crib board.

"Oh, that!" Katie said. "We decided to race down the trail."

Rusty had to admire her answer. It was no lie. They did decide to race down the trail, but not against each other.

"Who won?" GJ asked, peering up at them over his reading glasses.

"We did!" Rusty blurted out.

Gram glanced up sharply. GJ put down his cards. Rusty thought quickly. "I mean, *she* did!"

"She who?"

"Sheila, of course. Sheila always wins."

GJ nodded. "I expect we'll be watching you at the Olympics one of these years, Sheila." He picked up his cards.

"Anyone for a game of Crazy Eights after I win this game?" Gram asked.

Rusty, Sheila and Katie glanced at one another. They looked at the picnic table and they looked at the road. "Sure," Katie said, "as long as we can play inside the trailer. It's kind of cold out tonight." She shivered.

"Cold? It's baking hot," GJ said in surprise.

"I'm cold too," Rusty said and gave his best imitation of a shiver, even though he was melting from the heat. "It cools down quickly up in the mountains, you know."

"I'm kind of cold too," Sheila admitted. "But before we start the game, can we go over to the shower building? Katie really needs a shower if you ask me!"

Everyone laughed—except Katie.

They walked the short distance to the showers, women's on one side of the building, men's on the other. After long, cool showers, they were ready to stay inside for an entire game. Anything beat sitting outside in full view of the road.

Later, before they crawled into their tents, Katie reminded Sheila and Rusty, "Don't anyone dare go to sleep before midnight. We need to watch and see if any more of Rusty's *ghosts* go creeping past."

Inside his tent, Rusty propped himself up on his pillow and watched the shadowy road. He fought to keep his eyes from closing.

Two smells tickled his nostrils. Two very familiar smells. The friendly aroma of brewing coffee was all but lost in the sharp scent of burnt toast. A robin chirped overhead but was immediately drowned out by screaming crows. Rusty yanked his sleeping bag from over his eyes. Bright sunlight flooded the campsite. He yawned and stretched and crawled outside.

"It's about time you woke up," Gram said. She and GJ sat at the picnic table, their little propane campstove perched nearby with a coffee percolator gurgling happily on one burner. On the other burner their camp toaster spouted tendrils of smoke. Two pieces of toast lay side by side like chunks of charred wood, and a crow hopped a little nearer on a cottonwood branch, eyeing the toast and cawing loudly.

GJ raised his coffee mug. "Gram peeked into the girls' tents to be sure they were actually there," he said. "You three slept in for so long we were beginning to worry."

"So—you didn't care about me?" Rusty asked, rubbing his fingers through his tousled red hair. "Just Katie and Sheila?"

Gram laughed. "We didn't need to check your tent. We could hear you snoring from inside the trailer."

"I don't snore."

"Tell that to the big old black bear who came snuffling around to see what all the noise was about early this morning."

"Jerry! Don't scare the boy!" Gram turned to Rusty. "It's not true, your grandfather's kidding." She grinned. "We only *thought* we heard a bear when we first woke up, but it turned out to be you, snoring."

Rusty opened his mouth to protest, but changed his mind. "I'm going in to get dressed." He limped toward the trailer. His heel hurt more now than it did the night before

By late morning they were back in Barkerville. Gram consulted the schedule of events. "We've missed this morning's guided tour of the town," she said. "And the schoolhouse demonstration has already started. If we run the entire distance to Richfield, we might catch Judge Begbie's session in the courthouse."

"But it's uphill all the way," GJ pointed out. "Aren't all those demonstrations on again this afternoon?"

Gram nodded. "But I want to see the show at the Theatre Royal today."

"Fair enough, but there's always tomorrow. How about walking up the trail to the cemetery at Camerontown?"

"Gee—that sure sounds like fun." Katie wrinkled her forehead. "Nothing like visiting a whole pile of dead guys."

"I want to see Billy Barker's original mine," Rusty said. "This entire town was built around the shaft where Barker first stuck paydirt back in 1862, so it's kind of important."

"Listen," GJ told them, "if you kids promise not to let each other out of your sight and to stay inside the town, you can visit where you want while Gram and I walk up to the cemetery."

After agreeing to meet in front of the Lung Duck Tong Restaurant at 12:30, Rusty and the two girls set off on their own. Finally they had a chance to talk privately.

"So, Rusty," Katie asked, "did you see him again?"

"Who? Three Finger?" He shook his head. "Did you?"

"No," Katie admitted. "I fell asleep."

"Me too," Sheila said, "right after Rusty started snoring."

Rusty didn't object. If everyone thought he snored, it could be they were right. After all, he was asleep at the time, so how was he to know?

They started down the main street, Sheila with her nose in a tourist map. They were passing W.D. Moses' barbershop when she said, "If we cut through here, between the barbershop and Dr. Watt's office, we can see where the fire started. At least, I think we can."

Rusty studied her suspiciously, wondering if Sheila had developed a sudden interest in history. "Okay, what's the catch?"

"No catch, just a monument."

They made a sharp left turn onto short grass between the two small buildings and soon found themselves on Barkerville's back street.

"Well, I don't know." Sheila glanced around. "I thought it was here."

"Look, over there!" Rusty pointed to a small wooden sign stuck in the grass between the Wake-Up Jake and the barbershop. Katie ran over and Rusty limped behind her.

The sign explained that on the night of September 16, 1868, most of Barkerville was destroyed by fire. "I already knew that," Rusty said. "People think it started in Barry and Adler's Saloon, so that's where we should go next, to Barry and Adler's. Let's see the map."

They glanced around. "Where's Sheila?" Katie asked.

There was no sign of her. They returned to the quiet back street and looked up and down. "There she is!" Rusty pointed down the road where Sheila was leaning on a fence in front of a paddock, watching some big, handsome horses with gleaming brown coats.

"Somehow I didn't think she had a burning desire to see where the fire started," Rusty chuckled. "Get it? Burning des—"

"Shh!" Katie warned, staring in the opposite direction. "Look!"

Across the grass, beyond the wooden sign, a thin figure scurried out from between two tall, narrow buildings.

"It's Frizzy Hair." Rusty whispered. Her shoulders were stooped forward, just as yesterday, as if she were clutching something close against her stomach. She skimmed over the grass, cutting behind the Kelly House Bed & Breakfast. "What's she doing?" Rusty whispered. "Stocking up on Hair Invigorator?"

"As if she needs it! Come on, if we run we can catch up to her at the corner."

Katie darted along the back street, passed three small buildings and reached the corner at the same time as Frizzy Hair. Katie slowed to a walk and Rusty caught up.

"Hi!" Katie grinned. "Did you find some more Hair Invigorator this morning?"

Frizzy Hair stopped short. Her narrow eyes flicked from Katie to Rusty. Jerking her head back to flick away hair that floated over her forehead in the breeze, she pulled three tall bottles closer against her stomach.

"We saw you yesterday. At the barbershop," Katie reminded her. "So we just wondered if you found some more bottles of Hair Invigorator that magically appeared on the shelf."

"It must be good stuff!" Rusty said, eyeing her hair.

"I'm sure it is," Frizzy Hair said sharply. She edged around them, turned, ran across the street and hurried up the path to a building marked *Staff Only*. The door slammed shut behind her.

"She's going to look like a woolly sheep," Rusty said.

"Not necessarily. This time she had three bottles of whiskey."

Rusty pressed his hand hard against his forehead. He had the strongest feeling that the answer was right there, so close he could almost touch it. Then it snapped into his mind and he said, "Two bottles of Hair Invigorator from W.D. Moses' barbershop. Three bottles of whiskey from Barry and Adler's Saloon. Exactly the things that were stolen on those first two nights, just before Three Finger disappeared!"

For a long moment Katie stared at him, round-eyed. Then she took off at a run. Rusty followed. When he caught up, Katie was standing between the two tall buildings where they first spotted Frizzy Hair. She looked from one to the other. A fence linked the fronts of the buildings, blocking the way to the main street. While the building on their right had a side door, the one to their left had only a window.

"She must have come from there," Katie said, nodding toward the door.

Rusty nodded.

"So is this Barry and Adler's Saloon?" she asked.

"I don't know. Let's go get the map from Sheila."

As they neared the wooden sign, someone was standing with his back to them, reading about the fire. It was Prospector Man! They hurried on by, hoping he wouldn't notice them.

They found Sheila still at the fence, stroking the muzzle of a large horse. "Isn't he beautiful?" she asked.

"Sure, beautiful," Rusty agreed. "Where's the map?"

She handed it to him and he studied it as they walked in the opposite direction from Prospector Man. Katie told Sheila what had happened.

"There is no Barry and Adler's anymore," Rusty said. "It wasn't restored. Madame Bendixen's Saloon and Boarding House is the closest saloon to where the fire started, and that's where we saw Frizzy Hair."

Katie nodded. "I think someone left the whiskey bottles there last night and Frizzy Hair took them, just like she took that hair stuff."

"That doesn't make any sense," Sheila objected. "Why would anyone go sneaking around putting stuff back on the shelves?"

"I haven't figured out why yet, but I bet it's Rusty's Three Finger Ghost who's doing it. Remember when we saw him that first night? He was carrying something in a bag."

"It's Three Finger's ghost all right. It has to be!" Rusty said. "And that was him looking for his old cabin too, before Prospector Man sneezed. Three Finger has returned to make amends so he can rest in peace."

"Rusty," Katie told him patiently, "you're letting your imagination get away with you again. There has to be a logical explanation and we're going to find out what it is."

"Mark my words," Rusty said, "tomorrow morning four of those leather pouches for carrying gold nuggets will show up at Mason and Daly General Merchants."

"Shouldn't that be three?" Katie asked. "One of them was found at that Chinese apothecary's just after the fire."

"Right," Rusty nodded, "Eng Chung's. But anyway, we need to be at Mason and Daly's bright and early tomorrow morning."

"And today," Katie said, "after we get back, we have to go up Lowhee Trail and find that cabin."

Sheila made an odd, strangled sound in her throat.

11

A Letter and a Map

When they returned to their campsite that afternoon, Gram checked her watch. "We've got to hurry. Joyce Evans is expecting us at four o'clock."

Rusty could not imagine anything more boring than sitting around a campsite listening to three adults talk. And besides, he could hardly wait to get started on the search for Three Finger's cabin. "Do I have to go?"

"Of course not, Rusty, but GJ and I did see Ms. Evans leaving the Goldfield Bakery with a huge bag of goodies less than an hour ago."

"Mmm," Katie said. "I'm going. That bakery smells scrumptious."

"Me too." Sheila patted her stomach. "I'm hungry."

Rusty reconsidered. Now that he thought about it, he was kind of hungry, and his mouth watered just thinking about that bakery. But there was a stubborn streak in Rusty that wouldn't let him give in too easily. So he drew a deep breath, gave a mournful sigh. "Maybe I'll come."

"You don't need to bother," Katie told him. "I promise to bring you some leftovers—if there are any."

"Crumbs," Sheila added. "We'll bring you some crumbs and maybe a bit of icing sugar in the bottom of the bag."

Rusty ignored them and went to get *Spirits of the Cariboo*.

Joyce Evans was so intent on the map spread out on her picnic table, she didn't hear them arrive. At the far end of the table was a large pitcher of iced tea, six tall glasses. and a plate piled high with mouthwatering donuts.

"Hi, Joyce," Gram said. "Is that the map you were looking for?"

Ms. Evans jumped. Then she quickly folded the map. "It's kind of embarrassing actually. I found it on that little table." She nodded toward a folding table under her awning. "It was underneath a book, but I honestly don't recall putting it there."

Gram chuckled. "I wouldn't worry. I do things like that all the time."

"I brought my book," Rusty said, handing *Spirits of the Cariboo* to Ms. Evans.

"Thank you so much, Rusty. You know, since I arrived here, everyone has been talking about this book, but the gift shop hasn't one copy left." Ms. Evans gazed at the cover and ran her fingers over the photo of the half-visible man. "Would you mind if I borrowed it for a few hours? I promise to return it before dark."

"Fine with me."

Ms. Evans tucked her map and a folded sheet of paper inside the book, which she laid on the table. Then she poured iced tea for everyone.

Rusty, Sheila and Katie sat at the picnic table near the closed screen door of Ms. Evans' tent-trailer. The adults settled on folding chairs under the spreading branches of a cottonwood tree, nibbling on one small donut apiece, sipping their iced tea and chatting about boring stuff. Rusty turned his attention to the stack of donuts. He had an important decision to make. Which one was the biggest? He finally settled on a bear paw—a long, fat donut crammed with whipped cream and coated in dark chocolate. He took a huge bite. Awesome! He closed his eyes and lost himself in the sweet taste.

Someone kicked his shin. Not hard, but enough to make his eyes pop open. Whipped cream oozed from the remainder of his bear paw. He caught it with his tongue, just in time.

Another kick!

Across the table, Katie pulled a face at him. Her eyes flicked from him to the tent-trailer behind him and back again. Rusty looked over his shoulder and his jaw dropped. Just visible through the screen door was a pair of boots. They were unusually tall and quite different from your average modern-day leather boots.

"Uh, Ms. Evans," Katie asked, "could I have some more iced tea, please?" She picked up the empty pitcher. "I'll make it for you."

"Of course, help yourself," Ms. Evans said. "The mix is on the counter and the ice cubes, naturally, are in my little freezer."

"Come and help me, Rusty," Katie said.

Rusty stuffed the remainder of his bear paw into his mouth, hopped up and opened the screen door. He stared. On the floor in front of him were bootprints. Dusty, almost obliterated, but unmistakable. They were the same as the prints he had sketched.

Katie brushed past him. He stepped inside and closed the screen door. While Katie set about making more iced tea, Rusty glanced outside to be sure none of the adults could see, then picked up a boot and flipped it over.

"A perfect match," he whispered.

As he bent to put down the boot, Rusty glanced toward the small table near the door. Held down by salt and pepper shakers was a piece of yellowing paper. He looked closer. It was covered with scratchy, old-fashioned ink handwriting. He picked it up. Katie peered over his shoulder. They read quickly.

September 7, 1868

My Dearest Emily:

At last I am able to return to you and the children. I most sincerely apologize for leaving you alone these many years. You were quite right. I was being selfish. Nothing turned out as I had hoped.

I have lived in this wretched town for long enough, spent my last spring wading over a main street that becomes a raging river. Did I mention that all the buildings are set on stilts to allow spring floods to wash through?

Once here, my dreams of riches quickly shattered, as you know. Nevertheless, I was loath to return empty-handed. Knowing that you were forced to mortgage our farm in order to feed and clothe the children made returning even more difficult, especially since I always believed my fortune was waiting, just around the corner. However, rest assured, our troubles are over at last. I may not have struck gold, but I have managed to put aside a substantial fortune nevertheless. I dare not say more about it now, but will explain all in my final letter to you, which I am working on and will keep safely hidden, in that secret hiding spot I mentioned previously, until the time comes to leave. I shall mail the letter from Victoria and trust that it will arrive safely in Cornwall shortly before I, myself, get home.

I plan to leave my windowless little cabin for good by the end of this month and walk as far as Quesnel, keeping to the trails and back roads. I must confess to a strong feeling of foreboding. I expect this comes as a result of the many dishonest things I have done, and still must do, in order to return home. In the event that something terrible happens to me before I escape this hideous country, Kees has agreed to bring all my gear, which is little enough, when he leaves Cariboo for the winter. He will ship it out to you from Victoria. I trust Kees implicitly.

Until we meet again, my dearest Emily.
Your loving husband,
James

Rusty put the letter back. His eyes wandered to the bench seat and he jumped back in surprise.

Poking from beneath a bright pink cushion was something white and hairy. He reached out cautiously, lifted a corner of the cushion and then picked it up. Underneath was something that resembled a pure white Angora cat, squashed flat. At the sound of a soft footstep outside, Rusty dropped the cushion.

The screen door creaked open. By the time Ms. Evans' face appeared in the doorway, Rusty had opened the small, below-counter refrigerator. Katie picked up the full pitcher and grinned.

"Are you having problems finding things?" Ms. Evans asked.

"No," Katie said. "Rusty's always kind of slow. He daydreams, you know." She said this as if he suffered from an incurable disease.

Rusty busied himself plopping ice cubes into the tea while Ms. Evans waited. Outside, they rejoined Sheila, who had opened Rusty's book to the story of Three Finger. "Look at this," she said to Ms. Evans. "A man named James Evans came to Barkerville from Cornwall, just like you. Maybe you're related!"

"Actually, we are, but I learned about him only recently. He was my late husband's great-grandfather, and I can't say I'm proud to admit it."

"Oh?" Katie asked. "Why's that?"

"Thanks to him, this family has been cursed with tragedy for all these years," Ms. Evans said bitterly.

"Like what?" Rusty asked.

Her eyes filled with tears and she covered her mouth with one hand. "I'm sorry, I shouldn't have said anything." She hurried away.

Rusty poured himself a glass of iced tea, grabbed another donut and sat down beside Sheila, who lifted the front cover of the book as if trying to prevent him from seeing the page she was reading. Naturally he tried to peek over top. But Sheila's fingers tapped insistently on the table beside the book. He looked down and almost choked.

There, shielded from the adults' view, was the paper Ms. Evans had tucked inside his book. It was an old, hand-drawn map. Crisp and yellowed with time and crisscrossed with cracks from many foldings, the map showed a trail marked "Lowhee" that wound up the mountainside just north of Barkerville. Partway up, the trail split in two. A dotted line had been inked in parallel to the right-hand trail and stopped where a small creek trickled down the hillside. An X marked this spot, and from there the dotted line continued along the creek to a second X. Between the two X's was written "253 paces." At the second X the dotted line took a sharp turn to the right, indicating "57 paces" from there to a tiny drawing of a log cabin, complete with stone chimney and a curl of smoke. Printed below the cabin were the initials "J.E." Next to the chimney, printed neatly in ballpoint ink, was one word: "Gold?"

Rusty's mouth went dry. He reached for his iced tea. Katie was scribbling like mad, her head bent over her notebook. He assumed she was making notes about the letter they had just read. That gave him an idea. Pulling his sketchbook from his backpack, Rusty proceeded to sketch a copy of the map. When he was done, he slipped the original to Sheila and she tucked it back inside the book. They all stood up at once.

"Thanks, Ms. Evans," Sheila called. "Those donuts were delicious!"

Katie thanked her too and added, "I think we need to go for a hike up the trail now. I ate way too much!"

"Me too," Rusty said. "Thanks, Ms. Evans. I really pigged out!"

"I guess you won't be needing any dinner tonight then?" GJ asked.

"Trust me," Rusty said, "by the time we hike up that mountain and back down behind Sheila, we'll be hungry again!"

They hurried up the trail. When they reached a little creek, they stopped while Rusty retrieved his copy of Ms. Evans' map from his backpack, then unfolded and consulted it.

"I can't believe Ms. Evans is the ghost!" Sheila said.

"The man, you mean," Katie corrected her. "Or, I

should say, the woman dressed as a man dressed as a prospector from the past."

"Dressed as a ghost from the past," Rusty added. "The evidence is in her trailer."

"And evidence does not lie," Katie said. "Yesterday she was up here tramping around in the bushes, trying to find the cabin—which means she must think the gold is still here." Katie pulled out her notebook. "Three Finger's letter mentioned a hiding place. He said he told his wife about it in an earlier letter."

"Hey!" Sheila said. "When you two were snooping around in her tent-trailer, Ms. Evans told Gram and GJ that she sold the old family farmhouse in Cornwall last month. She said it took her, like, forever to clean out the attic because of all the old letters and stuff that were stored there for the last 200 years."

"All right!" Katie said. "If she has Three Finger's letters, she knows where the secret hiding place is."

"And she used Three Finger's map to find the exact spot." Rusty waved his map at Katie. "Look at what she wrote beside the chimney!"

"*Gold?* But before she found it, Prospector Man scared her off."

"And," Rusty said, "she might have been in the wrong spot. Think about it. Three Finger counted 253 paces from the trail. But you gotta remember, he was a small man, even for back then when the average person was shorter than today. Besides, he had three toes missing from one foot and a gimped-up leg."

"Which means," Sheila said, "his paces would be shorter than Ms. Evans'."

"So," Katie considered, "all we have to do is walk like we have a two-toed foot and a bad leg. Right?" She started to hobble toward the overgrown path.

"Both on the same side?" Sheila asked.

"Don't know," Rusty admitted. "But it doesn't really matter so long as we take smaller steps."

Sheila watched Katie slowly disappear up the streambed. "I have an idea," she said. "How about we each count separately and then search wherever we end up?"

"Okay," Rusty agreed. "You go now, and I'll wait a couple of minutes."

While he waited, Rusty searched the ground until he found a good stout stick the perfect size for a walking stick. Then he returned to the creekbed. *Okay. I need to concentrate now. If I lose count, I'll have to come all the way back.* He started up the hillside, thinking how lucky he was to have a heel that rubbed against his shoe and hurt more with every step so he didn't need to fake a limp. He stopped, turned around and limped the few steps back to the start of the trail. "Okay, here goes, *concentrate:* one, two, three, four, five, six..."

"...249, 250, 251, 252, 253." He stopped and looked around. The land here sloped steeply up from the creek-bed.

The only sound was the rush of wind in trees high above his head. His heel hurt so much now, he decided to take a brief rest, leaning on the walking stick. He realized there was no point in searching here, because no one would build a cabin on such a steep slope. Just ahead, though, the ground leveled off. He hobbled to that spot, turned right, away from the stream, and counted fifty-seven paces. Here was the perfect spot to build a log cabin. Flat ground, water close by—even if it was only a trickle. Rusty removed his backpack and, using his walking stick to push aside dry leaves and prod through undergrowth, began his search.

Back and forth, up and down, he covered every inch of level ground. He found several good-sized, flat-sided rocks, perfect for building a chimney, but never more than two or three together. He wondered if the girls were having better luck, but decided that if either of them found anything, they would let him know. Discouraged, he sat down on a fallen tree to take a drink from his water bottle.

The trunk he sat on was about two feet in diameter and covered in moss. Young trees sprouted from the old bark. A ball of gnarled and twisted roots reached high above his head. Rusty gazed idly up at the roots as he drank. Wedged tightly among them were dozens of rocks of various sizes, rocks that had been yanked out of the ground years earlier when the tree toppled over. He wondered how long this tree had been lying here. He wondered how old it was. Eighty years? One hundred? He had no idea. All he knew was that none of the trees up here grew as big as the giant cedars and Douglas firs on the coast. Could this tree have been a young sapling when Three Finger built his cabin? He stared.

The wood of the one-room cabin, smaller than their trailer, would slowly deteriorate over time. When the cabin collapsed, its chimney would likely tumble down. Seedlings would sprout in the rotten wood, moss would creep over the chimney rocks. Seeds would land in that moss and also begin to sprout. If a tree started growing on a pile of rocks, its roots would eventually break up the pile. But the tree would be at a definite disadvantage with its roots above ground, searching around rocks to find nourishing soil and water. Eventually, outgrown by surrounding trees, it might simply topple over and die, lifting the chimney rocks up with its roots.

Rusty slid off the fallen tree trunk and ran to the bottom end of the root ball.

12

A Map and a Curse

Rusty brushed his fingers over one of the rocks stuck among a tangle of roots. A grayish blue soil clung to his fingers. When he rubbed them together it felt soft and chalky. Excited now, he recalled Mustache Man mentioning a layer of blue clay below the gravel of Williams Creek. Could Three Finger have used the clay as mortar for his chimney?

Rusty started yanking moss by the handful away from the ground at his feet. He stopped and stared, scarcely able to believe his luck. Beneath the moss lay a cluster of smooth, egg-shaped rocks, roughly the size of baseballs. He lifted one out, then another and another. "Hey!" he yelled. "Hey! I think I found it!"

Someone might have answered, he couldn't be sure, but he was too excited to call again. He picked up rocks, one after another, expecting underneath each one to find a tin box bursting with gold.

"What makes you think it's here?"

Rusty jumped. He had not heard the girls approach.

"There's blue clay here, not the usual soil for a forest floor. And look at all these smooth river rocks piled in one place. This used to be a chimney, I'm sure of it!"

The girls got down to help.

Ten minutes later, Sheila shouted, "Look!" She pointed at a large rock below Rusty's foot. The corner of something poked out, something bright and shiny. Rusty tugged at it, but it wouldn't come loose.

Sheila helped him roll the rock aside. Wedged in a space between two lower rocks lay a disappointingly small, rather battered hunk of tin. Rusty dug his fingers into the clay holding it, but the tin was firmly stuck. "My Swiss Army knife!" he yelled. "It's in my backpack."

When Katie handed it to him, Rusty carefully worked the blade around the tin until it came free. The tin box was about four inches long by two inches wide and a half inch deep. "It must be a really small fortune," he said, working at the lid. When it wouldn't come off, he pried it with his knife. His heartbeat quickened as he reached inside, expecting to find gold nuggets. Instead, he pulled out a neatly folded sheet of paper. His fingers shook as he unfolded it. Although it was obviously old, the paper had been well preserved inside the dry tin box. "It's another letter!"

Katie and Sheila peered over his shoulders. "It's Three Finger's last letter!" Katie said. "The one he was planning to mail from Victoria."

September 5, 1868

My Dearest Emily:

By the time you receive this letter, I shall not be far from home, as it will have been mailed from Victoria the day I arrive. I believe it is safe to explain here what has happened, without fear of my words falling into the wrong hands on the long Cariboo Wagon Road from Barkerville. Not being a brave man, I find it easier to explain in writing than to your face.

Although the pay for working in the mines is low, I have found it occasionally possible, over the past year, to make off with gold nuggets of varying sizes and values. No one knows this other than you. I don't dare tell even my very good friend, Kees. You might wonder at this, as I have said I would trust Kees with my life, but the truth is I am ashamed of what I have done and fear Kees would think less of me as a man.

The mine owners are increasingly suspicious, but whenever they have cause to believe a gold nugget has gone missing, they blame a Chinese worker and fire the lot of them on the spot. The first time this happened, as you can imagine, I felt horribly guilty. However, they were all hired back again because they are such good workers and are paid only half of what a white man makes. This of course is unfair, but that is how things work up here.

None of this excuses what I have done in order to return home safely. Please, my dear Emily, do not be too harsh in your judgment of me. I have done this for my family and intend to work until my dying day if necessary to pay back every cent I have taken.

Over the past year, I hid my gold nuggets in two tin boxes, both of which are concealed in the shaft of that same abandoned mine where I fell and broke my leg last year. That fall is what finally did me in. I knew then that I would never earn enough honest money to return home. I began saving from that time.

On the day I leave, I shall not show my face in Barkerville again, but simply collect the gold and continue up Stout's Gulch Trail to begin my long journey home. Meanwhile, I shall keep this letter well hidden.

I am adding this brief note because I am so excited! Only a few days now. I have needed to borrow a few necessary items from Barkerville's merchants over the past three nights. I cannot very well walk in and pay for these things with my stolen gold nuggets because the merchants would immediately become suspicious. Already they do not trust me.

One day, when the time is right, I shall repay them all and more as well. In the meantime, I expect they will blame the Chinese, and most especially one Eng Quan, for the thefts. For that, too, I must one day make amends.

Your loving husband,
James

"If he never mailed his letter," Sheila said, "that means he never made it to Victoria."

"He never even left Barkerville," Katie pointed out, "or he would have taken the letter with him. So something happened to him before he could collect his gold."

"And it's still sitting in that abandoned mine," Sheila said, "by Stout's Gulch—wherever that is."

While the girls talked, Rusty held the tin box to the light and peered inside. Something else was stuffed in the bottom. A piece of crumpled paper? He stuck his fingers in but could not quite reach it. Holding the tin upside down, Rusty used his Swiss Army knife to work the paper out. He unfolded it. "Hey! Look at this!"

It was a small, hand-drawn map that showed the Richfield Trail. About halfway to Richfield, a dotted line veered off to the southwest, up Stout's Gulch. At a place labeled Emory Gulch was a small X, and from there the dotted line continued up Stout's Gulch for "287 paces" to a second X. Then it veered "due west" for "346 paces" and ended at a little square labeled "Abandoned Mine Shaft."

"Let's go!" Katie said.

"We can't go up there now," Rusty told her. "The Richfield Trail is on the other side of Barkerville."

"Rusty's right," Sheila agreed. "It's too late today and too far to go."

Katie's shoulders slumped. "All right—tomorrow then. We'll find a way to get up there tomorrow, right after we check out Mason and Daly's store to see if those leather pouches come back."

They hurried down Lowhee Trail and had just passed the fork when they ran around a bend and saw a small white-bearded figure heading uphill toward them. Head bent, he walked quickly and didn't see the kids until they were almost upon him. Then his thin brown eyebrows raised and his soft blue eyes opened wider. But he quickly put his head down again and scurried past. Rusty recognized those eyes and knew for certain who it was.

They continued down the trail single file, with Sheila in the lead and Rusty, as usual, lagging behind. Ahead, from around the next bend, they heard a muffled sneeze. Moments later a second white-bearded prospector came in sight. Prospector Man's eyes were on the trail and hidden beneath the brim of his hat; the sleeves of his red-and-black-checked shirt were rolled up to the elbows. Rusty took a good look at his beard. It might be a fake, but it was a good fake, and it looked exactly like the other one.

Prospector Man glanced up sharply. "You three! Again?" he growled. They clustered together. Prospector Man was not tall, but he was strongly built with broad, muscular shoulders. "And just what do you think you're doing up here?"

Rusty's heart stopped. His throat seized up.

"Simply enjoying nature," Katie told him. "This *is* a public trail."

Prospector Man planted his feet wide apart, placed his hands on his hips and glared down at Katie. "Why are you spying on me?" he demanded.

Rusty noticed red scrapes, cuts and bruises on Prospector Man's arms. No wonder he was so angry. "Why are you following that other prospector guy?" he heard himself ask.

Prospector Man swung around and stepped so close the toe of his heavy boot crunched down on Rusty's sneaker.

"Ow!"

Beneath his dark, bushy eyebrows, the man's slate gray eyes narrowed. He shook a finger at Rusty. "Listen. I will say this only once so you better pay attention!" He opened his mouth, drew a deep breath and sneezed in Rusty's face.

"Oh! Gross!"

"If I ever, I mean *ever,* catch any of you spying on me again, I will teach you a lesson you'll never forget!" Prospector Man pulled a tissue from his pocket and blew his nose with a honk like a ferry horn. "These trails can be dangerous, remember. More than one prospector has been lost between here and Quesnel." With that he pushed Rusty out of his way and continued up the trail.

"Now what?" Rusty whispered. "I am sure that was Ms. Evans we passed before. He's following her. We need to warn her."

"He won't hurt her," Katie said confidently. "He's waiting for her to find the gold."

"And she won't find it," Rusty said, "because we will! Tomorrow!"

They hurried down the trail, Rusty limping worse than ever because his toes hurt now as much as his heel.

"There was a letter with the map," Sheila said when they reached the campground.

Katie frowned. "We know, we were there, remember?"

But Sheila shook her head. "No. I mean with that map Ms. Evans tucked into Rusty's book."

"What? Why didn't you tell us before?"

"Because I knew you'd want to open it, and Ms. Evans would notice because it was folded in four and the paper is super flimsy."

"Let's go check it out." Katie started along the back road.

"We can't go into her tent-trailer!" Sheila said firmly. "That's private property."

"But what if it's still in the book on the picnic table?"

"The book's my property," Rusty said. "I think that's legal."

Sheila looked doubtful.

"We'll just walk past her campsite, okay?" Katie said. "And see if the book is there. If it isn't, we won't go in, I promise."

At the far end of the back road they walked quickly past Prospector Man's campsite. His white van was still parked in the same spot. There was no one in sight. They continued around the curve and stopped at the entrance to Ms. Evans' campsite. Her picnic table was empty.

"Let's get out of here," Sheila said, "like you promised."

"But look." Katie pointed at the small folding table pushed up against the tent trailer, under the awning. On it was Rusty's book. "That counts." Katie walked boldly into the campsite. She picked up the book, carried it to the picnic table, opened it and waved a folded sheet of paper at Rusty and Sheila. They ran to see.

Katie carefully spread the fragile paper on the table. Like the two letters from James Evans, the handwriting that covered two sides of this paper was in ink. This writing, however, was neat and precise.

October 12, 1868

Dear Mrs. Evans:

As Bishop of Saint Saviour's Church, Barkerville, I am honored that Mr. van der Boorg trusts me to write this letter on his behalf. Although he has learned to speak English very well, he has not had occasion to learn to write the language.

The following words are Mr. van der Boorg's.

I regret to tell you that your husband, Three Finger, has disappeared without a trace. I tried to find him. Here is all I know:

Three Finger left his backpack and everything he owns near his cabin. He met me for a whiskey to warm his insides before he started for home. But suddenly a fire broke out and this town burned to the ground.

That night I heard some men talking by Williams Creek. They said Three Finger started the fire and they were getting rowdy. So I set off to warn your husband. But he was not at his cabin and I could not find him.

I must warn you that Eng Chung is very angry at Three Finger. This old Chinese man thinks it is Three Finger's fault that his son, Eng Quan, got killed. I have been told Eng Chung used his ancient medicine to put a curse on your family.

The truth is that Eng Quan stole some gold nuggets. The evidence is clear. A leather pouch with gold dust in it was found under Eng Chung's back stairs. Then Eng Quan ran away. This proves he is guilty. I do not know why his old father believes it is Three Finger's fault, but I know my good friend is an honest man.

One of the miners who went looking for Three Finger said Eng Chung's curse caused Three Finger to die on September 16. It looks like this is true. This miner also told me that since the next day was Three Finger's forty-second birthday, Eng Chung would curse the number one son of Three Finger and every son's number one son to die on the day before he reaches forty-two.

This curse will not end until all the stolen items are returned and Eng Quan's name is cleared. Sadly, I do not know how this can happen when we both know Three Finger cannot be guilty.

Some people believe they saw Three Finger's ghost at night, but that was only me. I tried to solve this mystery so Eng Chung would take back his curse. But I have failed. I am so very sorry. I am an honest man but not educated.

With this letter I am sending you all the worldly possessions of your departed husband. You will see I have not opened his pack.

Your humble servant,
Kees van der Boorg

"Yikes!" Rusty said. "A curse upon the whole family."

"Hmm," Katie placed the letter on the open book, "doesn't Ms. Evans have a son?"

"Yes," Sheila said. "She was talking about him when you two were doing your snooping thing. And she said something about her son's birthday coming up soon."

"How old is he?" Katie asked.

Sheila shrugged. "How should I know?"

"Shh!" Rusty whispered. "Listen!"

At first the sound was faint, unrecognizable. Then came the loud *rrrrh-whump* of a van door sliding open. It was followed by a harsh cough.

13

Books, Beards and Boots

"Let's get out of here," Rusty whispered. "Prospector Man's watching us!"

"How could he be?" Katie asked. "We just saw him up on Lowhee Trail."

"Well...but...whoever's over there will see us snooping around Ms. Evans' campsite. He'll tell her!"

"What if *he's* snooping around Prospector Man's van? *We* might tell on *him*."

Sheila gave an exasperated sigh. "Just don't look," she said. "Close the book and walk away. Now." Without waiting for a reply, she headed for the road.

All the tiny hairs on the back of Rusty's neck stood on end. He really wanted to leave, but Katie leaned on the picnic table, fingering the letter, lost in thought. "Leave it, Katie, let's get out of here!"

Whether it was his excellent advice or another cough from the campsite behind that helped Katie make up her mind, Rusty did not know. He didn't much care, either. He was so relieved to see her tuck the letter inside the book.

They joined Sheila on the road and walked quickly away. The little number sign in front of their own campsite beckoned to them, and Rusty could hardly wait to get there. But Katie stopped abruptly. "We need to go back."

Sheila groaned. "What now?"

"We can't leave the book on the picnic table. Ms. Evans will know someone was snooping."

"So?" Rusty asked. "She won't know it was us. And—knowing her—she probably won't even remember where she left it."

"I think she will." Katie looked up at the sky. "See all those clouds rolling in? I bet she moved your book in case it starts raining before she gets back."

"She still won't know it was us," Sheila pointed out.

"She will if the man in the van tells her."

"If you ask me," Sheila said, "I think she should lock things inside her tent-trailer when she leaves. Which means if we leave the book on the table, we're really doing her a favor—maybe she'll be more careful from now on."

Rusty felt a cold splatter on his nose, then another on his hand. He glanced up. "Unless a humungous bird just flew overhead, it's starting to rain. And I don't want my book to get wet."

They turned around. When they reached the entrance to Ms. Evans' campsite, they stopped and stared. The book was not on the picnic table.

"It moved!" Rusty pointed to the table beneath the awning.

"Maybe that van man moved it for her when he noticed the rain," Sheila suggested.

"Which means," Rusty pointed out, "that he *did* see us and he *will* tell her for sure."

"Look!"

They followed Katie's gaze to the white van's rear window, clearly visible through a gap in the trees. The one-way glass acted like a mirror. In the reflection they could see the picnic table, part of a man's head and a glimpse of his shoulders. He wore a blue baseball cap and had chubby cheeks. His head was bent and small glasses perched on the tip of his nose. Suddenly he glanced at the sky and pushed himself up from the table. He gave a loud, wheezy cough and hurried for the van, clutching a sheet of paper.

By the time they reached their campsite, it was pouring rain. GJ carried their portable barbecue from the picnic table and placed it under the awning. Gram grabbed towels and bathing suits from the line they had rigged up.

"Hey, kids! I'm glad you're here!" GJ said. "It looks like we're in for a downpour. You'd better put your tents away before they get too wet."

Rusty, for one, thought this was an excellent idea. He hated to be first to admit it, but he did not want to sleep outside tonight. With their three little white tents all in a row, clearly visible from the road, he wondered how long it would take before Prospector Man realized the three kids were sleeping inside those tents and decided it was a perfect opportunity to teach them a lesson they'd never forget.

That evening, instead of Crazy Eights, they played a board game around the table inside the trailer while rain pounded on the metal roof. Shortly after nine there was a knock on the door and GJ went to open it. "Joyce!" he said. "Come on in out of the rain."

Ms. Evans stepped inside wearing a waterproof jacket with her arms wrapped tightly against her stomach. "I brought your book back, Rusty," she said and pulled it from under her jacket. She handed it to Rusty while GJ took her jacket and hung it on a peg near the door.

"Please, sit down," Gram invited, "and I'll make you some tea." She got up to fill the kettle. "Are you feeling all right, Joyce?"

Rusty looked more closely at Ms. Evans and noticed how her wet face looked pinched and drawn. She pulled a white cotton handkerchief from her pocket and wiped her cheeks, but her eyes were red-rimmed and she looked exhausted.

"I am a bit tired," Ms. Evans admitted. She sank onto the couch and fidgeted nervously with her handkerchief. "I haven't slept well since arriving here."

"Did you drive all the way from Cornwall by yourself?" Rusty asked.

Ms. Evans nodded. "I'm quite used to being on my own since my husband died thirty years ago. Ted was crop-dusting our fields when his plane crash-landed in a drainage ditch. He was killed instantly." She hesitated and her lower lip wobbled. "When I heard the news, I was busy planning a birthday party for him, for the next day. He would have turned forty-two."

Rusty glanced at the others. "Do you have any children?" Katie asked quietly.

Ms. Evans nodded. "Two sons. They were just little boys then, of course. Scott, my older son, was not yet twelve when his father died—about your age, Rusty. Losing his father was very difficult for him."

Rusty added up the figures. Thirty years ago, almost twelve. "So Scott is forty-two now?"

"Not quite." Ms. Evans dabbed at her eyes with the handkerchief. "His birthday is next week." She sighed.

"And Scott has an eleven-year-old son of his own, named Brandon. Those two have such wonderful times together—they are off on a fishing trip in Northern Ontario right now." She stood up abruptly. "Listen, I really am exhausted. Thanks so much for the offer, but if you don't mind, I'll take a rain check on that tea, splash my way back to my trailer and go right to bed."

Ms. Evans slipped into her jacket and was about to open the door when she turned back. "By the way, Sheila, did you happen to notice a small, folded piece of paper when you were looking through Rusty's book this afternoon?"

"Paper?" Sheila glanced at Katie and away. "Uh, yes. It was still there when I closed the book."

"Strange." Ms. Evans bit her lip. "It seems to be missing now." She pushed open the door and stepped out into the gloomy, wet evening.

That night, as he lay in his sleeping bag on the fold-out couch, Rusty thought about Prospector Man and Ms. Evans in her prospector's disguise. She must have found Kees van der Boorg's letter in her attic last month and learned about the curse. So of course she would worry about her son, and that would explain why, after 136 years, she wanted to return all the stuff Three Finger stole.

Maybe they were wrong about the gold. Maybe Three Finger *did* manage to smuggle it out of Barkerville. Maybe it was in his pack when van der Boorg shipped it home to Cornwall. And that could mean Joyce Evans had a load of gold nuggets to return. Was that why Prospector Man kept spying on her? To get the gold? But how could he possibly know?

And who was that other guy in Prospector Man's campsite? He must have taken that letter out of the book, but why? Was he in cahoots with Prospector Man? Suddenly Rusty remembered when he and Katie went into Prospector Man's campsite to check out that map. Something or someone had made a noise inside the van. Did Prospector Man have a partner? These thoughts circled round and round in his mind as he grew more and more confused. But through all his confusion, one thing remained clear: first thing in the morning they would go straight to Mason and Daly's store.

Rusty's eyes opened slowly, lazily. Someone was standing over him. He jumped. Prospector Man?

"Relax, Rusty, I didn't mean to wake you. I'm just going to make some coffee."

Rusty remembered then. He was not in his tent, but safe inside the trailer where Gram was just now opening the blinds behind the stove. "The rain has stopped for now," she said, "but it's a perfect day to drive into Quesnel for groceries."

Rusty sat bolt upright. "We can't go to Quesnel today!"

His grandmother turned around, surprised. "We need a few things, Rusty. You three eat way more than either GJ or I imagined. And we thought it would be a nice change, especially for the girls. History isn't exactly their thing, as you may have noticed."

"But we *have* to go to Barkerville!"

"We will, Rusty, tomorrow for sure. I know there are lots of things still to see, but don't worry, we'll get to them all."

"But..."

"Quesnel is only about an hour from here. We thought we'd spend some time there today. There are riverboat trips to take and trails to walk and the old Hudson's Bay Company log building is now a restaurant. We'll have lunch there."

Rusty moaned. It all sounded so tempting. But they absolutely had to see Mason and Daly's first thing this morning.

"Also," Gram continued, "GJ wants to have the truck looked at before we haul the trailer out of here. He thinks the brakes might need some work."

"But..."

"Don't be selfish, Rusty. I know the girls would like a change. They haven't complained about spending time in Barkerville, have they?"

"No," Rusty admitted. Then it hit him, the perfect way out of this. *The best defense is the element of surprise*—at least that's what his dad always said. "Okay then, let's ask them. If Katie and Sheila want to go to Quesnel today, then you won't hear one word of complaint from me."

Gram searched his face. "Promise?"

"I'll go willingly, with a big happy grin."

To Gram and GJ's amazement, both girls were adamant that they wanted to spend the day in Barkerville.

"All right then," Gram agreed. "GJ and I need to go, but we'll just do the shopping, have the truck checked over and come back as soon as possible. You kids can go to Barkerville, but only if Joyce Evans agrees to drive you. She was planning to spend the day there and I'm certain she won't mind, especially since we already asked her over for dinner tonight. That way, if you run into any problems, you can go to her."

"But remember," GJ said sternly, "the three of you have to promise to stick together, just like yesterday, and stay inside the town limits."

"What about Richfield?" Rusty asked. "Can we walk up to Richfield? I want to see Judge Begbie's court."

"That shouldn't be a problem," GJ agreed.

"Now," Gram warned, "don't give Ms. Evans a bad time."

"Who? *Us?*" Katie raised an eyebrow.

"Of course not," Sheila said.

Rusty shook his head. "No way."

No one in Ms. Evans' little red Jeep spoke as they left the campground. The silence lengthened as they neared Barkerville. Rusty glanced sideways at his cousin, expecting her to be full of questions, but it seemed she wasn't sure how to begin.

Ms. Evans solved the problem. "So, Rusty, I hear you're interested in history?"

"Yep! And especially your grandfather, Three Finger Evans."

"My husband's great-grandfather," she corrected.

"Did you know he stole a bunch of stuff—like Hair Invigorator, whiskey and leather pouches?"

Ms. Evans' fingers tightened on the steering wheel.

"Some people think his ghost wanders around at night," Katie added. "Now, I don't believe in ghosts, but I have to admit, we've seen a couple of old prospector types around here."

"More than one?" Ms. Evans' voice was high-pitched, her knuckles white.

Katie nodded. "One small thin one and another bigger one who always tags along behind."

Ms. Evans gasped. "But...are you sure?"

"Yes. They both have white beards, and..." Katie hesitated, then plunged right in, "we think the smaller one is you."

Ms. Evans hit the brake, then the gas pedal, and the car hopped along like a jackrabbit. "Your grandparents told me you were quite the detective, Katie, but what makes you think that?"

"Lots of things."

"Like the boots and the white beard in your trailer," Rusty said.

Ms. Evans drove for a moment in silence. "Those boots belonged to Three Finger Evans, did you know that? But the beard was my son's. Scott and his best friend, Danny, dressed up as old prospectors one Halloween years ago. I found some really authentic-looking beards for them at the theater where I worked."

"Why did you dress up like that?" Katie asked.

"I just... I didn't want to be recognized and questioned if anyone saw me wandering around at night. I figured if people thought they were seeing a ghost, they'd likely keep quiet about it or everyone would make fun of them, you know? Also, being an actress, I always like to get into the part I'm playing." She slowed to enter the parking lot. "But this other ghost, exactly what does he look like?"

Rusty described him and added, "He's mean, too. He told us to stay out of his way or he'd 'teach us a lesson we'd never forget'!"

"So," Katie asked, "are you going to return the gold soon?"

"If I can find it, believe me, I'll return it immediately."

"Maybe we can help," Rusty offered.

"No." Ms. Evans parked the car and switched off the engine. "I want you to stay out of this. That man you describe sounds dangerous."

14

Frizzy Hair

They walked with Ms. Evans along Barkerville's damp street as far as Saint Saviour's Church. "What do you three plan on doing this morning?"

"We want to see Mas..." Rusty began but was drowned out by Katie.

"We're going up the Richfield Trail," she said.

"Oh! Listen, why don't I treat you to some fresh-baked goodies at the Goldfield Bakery before you go? I can smell it from here."

Rusty could too. The rich aroma of fresh baking was overpowering. "All right! Thank you, I'm so-oo hungry!"

"We just finished breakfast," Katie objected, but she and Sheila followed close behind as Rusty walked beside Ms. Evans to the bakery.

"Aren't you going to have one?" he asked, selecting the biggest donut he could see.

Ms. Evans shook her head. "I'm afraid I can't eat as much as I used to. One donut and I'd be full for the entire day!"

They wandered outside. No sooner had they settled on a bench than Ms. Evans glanced at her watch. "Oh dear!" she said. "I've just remembered, I'm meeting someone down the road and I'm late already. Enjoy your donuts. I'll see you later!"

They watched her take off at a near run along the raised plank sidewalk, wearing a small backpack, jeans, a light jacket and white running shoes.

"Hmm," Sheila observed, "she sure was in a hurry to get rid of us. I wonder what she's up to?"

"If you ask me," Katie licked a whipped-cream mustache from her upper lip, "she's going to return those gold pouches while everything is quiet. She was way too tired to walk into Barkerville last night, in the rain. After that, she needs to return the gold before her son's birthday."

"But she doesn't have it," Rusty said.

"I know, and it's up to us to find it for her, whether she wants our help or not. I say we check out Mason and Daly's, then go up Stout's Gulch and find that abandoned mine shaft. If the gold is there, we'll bring it out and give it to her."

"And if it isn't?" Sheila asked.

"It will be," Katie said.

As he limped along Main Street behind the girls, Rusty thought about another eleven-year-old boy, on a fishing trip with his dad. He tried to imagine how he would feel if his own father were suddenly taken from him. Katie was right—they had to find that gold. And fast!

She wore a different dress, but Rusty recognized her immediately. Her frizzy hair and squashed-bird hat were unmistakable. Her small gray eyes narrowed suspiciously when the three of them walked into Mason and Daly's. Rusty tried to ignore her, but his eyes were drawn against his will. He suppressed a gasp. Her hard, cold stare sent a shiver down his spine, and he pulled his eyes away to examine the large, cluttered room.

No space was wasted. Shelves crammed with clothing, boxes, hats and all manner of unusual items lined the walls. Pots, pans and huge woven baskets were suspended from the ceiling on hooks. Furniture, arranged in haphazard fashion, covered much of the floor space, while jackets and coats hung on racks.

His survey stopped at the small, rectangular window. Three brown leather pouches were lined up side by side on the sill. He started toward them, but was shoved roughly aside as Frizzy Hair dashed ahead of him and scooped up the pouches.

A plump young man wearing a suit jacket, bow tie, breeches and high boots stepped from the back of the store. "Phyllis! What brings you here so early?"

Frizzy Hair, or Phyllis, pulled the pouches close against her full skirt, hidden from the young man. "Just doing my rounds, Jason. I like to be certain everything is in order." She scooted out the door before anyone could say another word.

Rusty followed her, with Sheila close at his heels. Frizzy Hair sprang down the stairs so fast she tripped on her skirt, caught herself and darted across the street, her fine hair floating like a dark cloud around her head. She kept her left arm straight down, hiding the pouches in the folds of her full skirt until she disappeared into a short alley between the Theatre Royal and the Barkerville Hotel.

"She's heading for the staff-only building again," Rusty said. They darted around the corner of the hotel and skidded to a stop.

Frizzy Hair was standing in the middle of the road talking to two men Rusty recognized in a flash. They were the same two security guards he had overheard in Wake-Up Jake's!

Rusty and Sheila watched Frizzy Hair show them the pouches. "He's come back! Didn't I tell you? Three Finger is returning everything, just as I said he would.

Oh, how I would love to see him close up! He'll bring the gold back next, just you wait and see. And when he does, we'll be waiting for him."

"Now, Phyllis," the big guard said, "remember, we agreed to keep this quiet. Otherwise we'll be overrun with ghosthunters and golddiggers from all over the world. As if that *Spirits of the Cariboo* book won't cause enough trouble, now *you're* seeing ghosts too?"

Phyllis glanced nervously over her thin shoulder and her narrow eyes got narrower. "There they are! Those are the children who keep following me!"

The big guard noticed Rusty then. His eyebrows raised just slightly, but enough to tell Rusty that he recognized him. The man started toward them. "Want to tell us what you're up to?"

Rusty quivered in his sneakers. His throat seized up. He wanted to run, but his legs had turned to jelly. And then, to his horror, he heard himself say, "Actually, no."

The man stepped closer, so close Rusty could not see his angry eyes. He could see nothing but a tan button in the middle of a tan shirt.

Sheila grabbed Rusty's elbow and yanked him away. "We're simply touring Barkerville," she explained in a matter-of-fact voice. "That's what we came up here for. I hope it's not a problem."

"You can't go around harassing our staff members," the big guard said. He glanced at his partner. "Shall we take them in for questioning?"

"You can't do that," Sheila told him. "We didn't do anything wrong. I know the law, my mom's a police officer."

"Just don't cause any more problems," the smaller guard said. He smiled and his brown eyes looked friendly. "I'm David Eng," he added. "Tell me, why are you following Phyllis?"

Rusty began to relax. "Because she keeps taking all the stuff Three Finger returns. We want to know why."

"You see?" Frizzy Hair said. "I told you this boy saw Three Finger!" Her scowl miraculously vanished and her face crinkled into a smile. "Tell me, exactly what does he look like, son?"

"I, uh...he..." What was he supposed to say? Should he describe Joyce Evans in her Three Finger disguise or the other, bigger Prospector Man?

"I'm sorry," Sheila said, "but we're late for meeting our friend."

They walked quickly back toward the main street. "Where is Katie anyway?" Rusty whispered. But he no sooner asked than he saw her, waiting at the corner beside the Barkerville Hotel. She motioned them to hurry.

"Where were you?" Rusty asked.

"I saw Prospector Man again. He went into Mason and Daly's. And look over there!"

Across the crowded street, two people were standing in front of a carriage shed. One was Ms. Evans, the other was a chubby man wearing a blue baseball cap, dark blue sweatshirt and jeans. He had plump pink cheeks and his head was encircled by smoke from the pipe sticking out of his mouth. A blue and white sports bag slung over one stooped shoulder seemed oddly out of place.

"That's him!" Rusty whispered. "That's the man from Prospector Man's campsite. I bet he's telling Ms. Evans we were snooping around yesterday. Let's get out of here!"

"We can't go back," Sheila said. "I don't want to meet up with those two guards and Phyllis."

Before they could decide which way to turn, Ms. Evans glanced over and waved. "Hey, kids!" she called. "Come and meet Bill!"

They dragged themselves across the street. "Bill," Ms. Evans said, "these are my friends I told you about, Rusty, Sheila and Katie."

"You know, it was the strangest thing," Ms. Evans explained, "but last night, just after I left your trailer, I saw Bill splashing toward me in the rain. I could scarcely believe my eyes! You see, Bill's from Cornwall, just like me, and I know him because our two sons have been friends since they were kids. Also, it turns out his campsite is right behind mine, but we never noticed each other. Isn't that odd?"

Rusty looked up into Bill's round face. He wasn't a tall man, but he loomed above Rusty nevertheless. His smile was friendly enough as he reached out to shake Rusty's hand, but his slate gray eyes were hard and cold under his bushy white eyebrows. "Pleased to meet you," he said and squeezed so hard Rusty felt the bones in his hand crunch together.

"That's some coincidence," Sheila remarked as Bill turned to shake her hand.

Without stopping to think, Rusty reached out and grabbed Sheila's outstretched hand. "Sorry," he said to Ms. Evans, "but we're late. We're going up to Richfield."

He pulled Sheila away and Katie followed. They had gone about twenty steps before Sheila yanked her hand from his. "What was that about?" she demanded.

"Exactly what I want to know," Katie said. "I was planning to question him."

Rusty rubbed his aching right hand. With that and his sore foot, he was beginning to feel more like Three Finger Evans every day. "I think he broke my hand."

"What? Let me see." Katie grabbed his hand.

It looked quite normal in spite of how much it hurt. "He squeezed as hard as he could," Rusty explained. "He was going to hurt Sheila's hand too."

"Oh, wow! Thanks, Rusty," Sheila said as they hurried south along the street. They were passing the Lung Duck Tong Restaurant when Katie said, "So we know he knows."

"Who knows what?" Sheila asked.

"Bill knows we were in Ms. Evans' campsite, but he didn't tell her. Which proves he's up to no good."

"He's been spying on her from the back of his van," Rusty said. "That back window looks right into her campsite."

"Right," Katie agreed, "and it's one-way glass. He probably made sure she never saw him outside, even wearing his white beard."

Rusty was confused. "How many white beards are there?"

"Two. Ms. Evans' has one, and those two men take turns wearing the other one, depending on who is following her. The good thing is that now we know exactly who they are."

"Right," Rusty agreed, trying to sort things out in his mind. Two men who dressed alike, even to their white beards. They even had the same gray eyes. They stayed out of sight when Ms. Evans was at her campsite and took turns following her, wearing a disguise in case she spotted them. "But..." He noticed then that the girls were far down the road and scrambled to catch up.

As they started up Richfield Trail, Rusty kept trying to figure it out. One white beard, two men. If one was Bill, who was the other? Katie knew the answer. Even worse, she knew he didn't know. So, of course, he could never ask.

"Are we almost there yet?" Katie asked.

"Almost where?"

She raised an eyebrow. "To Stout's Gulch Trail!"

Rusty pulled the map from his backpack and unfolded it. "Not much farther."

They were still studying the map when someone appeared on the trail below. Prospector Man! He trudged up the trail, head bent, wide-brimmed hat hiding his eyes, a coil of rope over his shoulder. He saw them and his head jerked up, his jaw dropped.

Rusty waited for the man to yell at them, but he only scowled angrily and hurried on by.

"Just as I suspected," Katie whispered, "he's fol..."

Someone else came into sight. "Hi, kids!" David Eng called. "You'd better hurry if you're going up to Judge Begbie's courtroom."

As soon as the guard was gone they continued up Richfield Trail to Stout's Gulch Trail, which lead up the mountainside to their right. They darted up it before anyone else happened along.

15

Up the Gulch

"I really don't think we should do this," Sheila said. "It might be dangerous. Remember—"

"I know, I know," Katie interrupted, "you promised your mom not to cause trouble for Gram and GJ. But didn't you promise GJ we'd stick together?"

Sheila frowned.

"Besides," Rusty reminded her, "Ms. Evans needs our help."

Sheila rolled her eyes. "Oh, all right, I'll come—but only to keep you two from doing anything stupid."

"Whatever works!" Rusty grinned.

They stopped at a second, smaller gulch where it joined Stout's Gulch. "If this leads in from the southwest," Rusty said, "then it's got to be Emory Gulch."

"I'll check." Katie rummaged through her backpack and came up with a small plastic compass. "My dad made me promise to always keep this with me. He says

I have, like, zero sense of direction." She bent over the compass. "It's southwest all right. So we start counting here. How many paces?"

"287."

"Rusty," Sheila said, "you're the best at imitating Three Finger's way of walking. So you go first and we'll follow."

Rusty nodded, happy to be good at something. "I'll need a walking stick."

They spread out and searched the forest floor until Sheila called, "Got one!" She handed Rusty a good stout stick, just the right height to lean on.

"Ouch!" he said. "My hand hurts."

"Use your left hand," Sheila suggested. "Isn't it your left foot that's sore anyway?"

"Shh!" Katie put her finger to her lips. They listened, but heard only wind sighing through treetops. "I heard something on the trail below us, I'm sure of it."

"Probably just a falling fir cone," Sheila said.

"Let's get out of here!" Rusty leaned on the walking stick and repeated his peculiar, limping imitation of Three Finger's gait as he struggled up the steep slope. "One, two, three..."

At 287 paces he stopped. Just ahead a shallow ditch cut across the trail. Water from last night's rain trickled through the small channel and spilled over the bank to their right. On the high side, a narrow, rock-strewn swath zigzagged down the forested hillside. "This is it."

Katie checked the direction. "Due west," she confirmed, "let's go!"

The girls walked in front to push aside bushes and branches of trees, making it easier for Rusty to keep to his lopsided gait. But it was impossible to move quietly.

"...343, 344, 345, 346." He stopped. Looked around. In the shadowy light of a mature spruce forest there was little undergrowth, while high above their heads a steady wind rustled the canopy, masking other sounds.

"Now what?" Sheila asked.

"We search," Katie said. "I bet Three Finger covered the mine shaft with wood, just like that escape tunnel Rusty fell into near the old house in Victoria, remember?"

Rusty shuddered. How could he forget? He still had nightmares about it.

"So," his cousin continued, "be careful, because the wood must have rotted after all this time, and it will be covered with moss and stuff."

They searched in widening circles, taking slow, cautious steps, searching for any sign that a long-abandoned mine shaft led deep into the ground beneath their feet. Rusty felt ahead with his walking stick and tried to push away memories of that frightening fall.

"Let's try a little farther along," he suggested. "Remember, when we first stopped on Stout's Gulch Trail, we hadn't gone quite far enough."

As Rusty made his way through the trees, he thought about Three Finger Evans and felt a growing empathy for the old prospector who once hobbled along this same route, a big gold nugget hidden deep in his pocket. He stopped. What was that?

The ground trembled. An ominous rumble, deep beneath the ground, sent a shiver up through the soles of his feet. He held his breath. A creak, a groan and then an ear-splitting CRACK!

"AHHH!" Rusty threw himself to the forest floor, but the ground gave way beneath him and he felt himself sliding backward. It was happening again! He groped frantically for something to hold onto, something to slow his downward slide. But there was nothing. The end of his walking stick caught between two rocks, held, then began to slip away. His heart raced, his eyes squeezed shut.

He stopped sliding. Opened his eyes. Sheila had thrown herself on the ground and grabbed the only thing she could reach. His walking stick. She inched forward and latched onto his wrist. "Help me!" she yelled.

Katie appeared, flung herself down and grabbed his other wrist. Together they dragged him to safety.

"Congratulations!" Katie grinned and punched his shoulder. "You found it. You're good at stuff like that."

"Thanks," Rusty grumbled. He was trembling all over and determined not to go near that open shaft.

The girls edged over the loose gravel and peered into a gaping hole. "It's way dark," Katie said. She pulled her flashlight from her backpack. Sheila held her hand so Katie could lean closer and shine it down without falling. Katie took a good look, then both girls rejoined Rusty.

"It's only about five meters deep," Katie said, "and not very wide. Three Finger must have been really small if he fit in there."

"We need a rope," Sheila said.

"Maybe not," Rusty said. "Remember, Three Finger never told anyone about the gold, so he had no one to help him hide it. He didn't start stealing nuggets until after his accident, and he'd never be able to climb down there with his gimpy leg." He wouldn't want to, either, Rusty realized, after spending a long, scary night down there with a broken leg.

"Then," Katie reasoned, "he must have hidden his stolen gold near the top."

"If it was near the top," Sheila pointed out, "it would have gone down just now with that rock slide. We'll need to do some digging."

"I don't think so," Rusty said. "I figure Three Finger would use blue clay to make a hiding place for the boxes, just like he did for the map in his chimney. He'd make little nooks in the sides of the shaft, near the top, where he could reach them easily."

"Yes," Katie agreed, "but he'd need to hide the openings with loose rocks, just in case someone else looked in."

Sheila, being the least likely to fall headfirst into the shaft, volunteered to do the search. She stretched out on her stomach across the gravel with her arms free to reach into the mine shaft.

"You need to help me hold her ankles," Katie said.

Rusty stared at the loose gravel around the mine shaft and could not take a step closer. He shut his eyes. Falling. Tumbling into a deep, dark tunnel. Cold, slimy.

"Rusty?"

He opened his eyes. Katie was crouched on the gravel, holding Sheila's feet and looking up at him. "If she slips, I don't think I can hold her by myself."

Okay. Rusty swallowed. He had to do this. He took a deep breath, forced his fears into a distant corner of his mind and stepped closer. He crouched down, placed his walking stick at his side and held one of Sheila's ankles.

"You're right," Sheila's voice sounded hollow, "most of these rocks near the top are mortared in."

"Feel for loose ones," Katie whispered.

After some time, Sheila began to edge around the top of the shaft. The two cousins stayed with her, holding her ankles, keeping her safe. Rusty listened constantly, expecting at any second to hear heavy footsteps, to feel rough hands drag him away. He kept his walking stick close at his side.

Then he heard it. Behind him. A quick gust of wind? A twig crashing from the canopy? *A sneeze?* Before he could turn, there was a clink of rocks hitting together in front of him, deep within the mine shaft.

"I found something!" Sheila cried.

"Shh!" Katie warned.

Moments later, Sheila twisted around and sat up. Her face was bright pink as she inched forward, away from the mine shaft. In her hand was a square tin box the size of a box of chocolates. She opened it. They stared.

The box was more than half filled with coarse rocks, from green-pea size up to one almost as big as a golf ball. Some were light yellow, others were a more familiar deep gold and a few were darker, almost black. Rusty picked one up and held it on his palm. "Wow!"

"Let's get the other box," Sheila said. "I think it's farther back in the same little nook." Rusty put the nugget away and closed the tin box, which he placed next to his walking stick. He held Sheila's ankle again as she snaked forward to reach farther into the mine shaft. "Got it!" she cried.

"Shh!" Katie said again.

They sat together at the edge of the gravel while Sheila opened the second box. It was similar to the first, but heavier and crammed right to the rim with gold nuggets.

"Good work, kids!" said a gruff voice. "Now, if you'll just hand it over, we'll be on our way."

Rusty's heart flipped over. He looked up. And could not believe his eyes!

16

The Lure of Gold

Rusty expected to see Prospector Man, not Bill. And he sure as anything did not expect to see Ms. Evans! Something was horribly wrong. The two came from the direction of Stout's Gulch, but that sound—*that sneeze?*—had come from the opposite direction. He was sure of it.

The plump fingers of Bill's right hand rested firmly on Ms. Evans' shoulder as if he was her boyfriend or something. And she did not look happy. She seemed confused. He soon found out why.

"You kids knew where that gold was all along and didn't tell me?"

"We were going—" Rusty began, but Bill cut him off with a loud, wheezy cough.

The man's breathing was labored, every breath whistled eerily through his chest like a winter wind. And judging by the way Ms. Evans' shoulder sagged, Bill was leaning heavily on her. "I told you, Joyce." *Wheeze.*

"You're much too trusting." *Wheeze.* "I knew these kids wanted the gold for themselves." *Wheeze.* "They were acting mighty suspicious."

"Well, I don't know about that," Ms. Evans said, "but the important thing is that they found it." She gave a weak smile. "If you kids hand us the gold, Bill and I will take it to the security office and explain everything. I need to return it and clear Eng Quan's name as soon as possible."

Rusty, Sheila and Katie scrambled to their feet as Ms. Evans walked over to them. Rusty passed the box of gold to Katie and picked up his walking stick. He didn't like this. Not at all. And he could tell by the way Katie and Sheila edged away, each clutching a box of gold, that they didn't either.

"Please, Katie," Ms. Evans said, "Sheila. Please hand it to me. I need it, and Bill promised to accompany me into town to make sure the gold is safe."

"Don't trust him!" Katie warned. "He wants the gold for himself. Him and his son."

"Daniel is here too?" Ms. Evans asked, surprised.

"Of course not!" Bill shouted. He stood close behind Ms. Evans, breathing more normally now. "Have you seen him? You'd recognize Daniel—you've known him since he was a boy."

"Well, you know, it has been a long time since Danny and Scott used to play at the farmhouse together."

"Don't you think it's a huge coincidence that Bill shows up in Barkerville just when you're here?" Katie asked. "Here's what I think, Ms. Evans. I think your son, Scott, told his friend Daniel what you were planning to do. Daniel told his father and they decided to follow you and take the gold for themselves!"

They all heard it at once, the sound of a muffled sneeze followed by the rustle of tree branches behind them. Prospector Man emerged from the forest, blowing his nose on a tissue. "Darned allergies," he muttered. "The sooner I get away from these stupid trees the better."

"Danny?" Ms. Evans ran over. She reached up and pulled at his beard, which slipped below his chin. "I did notice you around Barkerville, but only because I thought your beard looked the same as mine. And of course it is! I bought them for you and Scott, remember? When you were boys." She frowned. "Danny, why are you here?"

Daniel avoided her eyes. "See—the thing is—we hate to see that gold wasted when it really should go to a worthy cause." He grinned at his father. "Like us!"

It hit Rusty that Daniel couldn't know about the curse, because if he did, he would help Ms. Evans, not get in her way. "Tell him about Eng Chung," he said. "Tell him how Three Finger Evans died the day before his forty-second birthday, and your husband did too!"

Ms. Evans sighed. "They aren't the only ones. I learned, from old papers in my attic, that James Evans, Three Finger's son, died in 1901. He was test-driving one of the first cars ever seen around Cornwall when he veered off the road into a ravine—the day before his forty-second birthday.

"James's son, Alan, was only an infant then, but he grew up to be my husband's father. Alan Evans was an air force pilot during World War II. He was old for a fighter pilot, I suspect, and may have lied about his age. He was shot down in 1941—the day before his forty-second birthday."

She glanced from Daniel to Bill. "You may recall that my husband, Ted, met a similar fate when he was crop-dusting our fields and crashed into a drainage ditch? Which means, including Three Finger, that's four first-born sons." She looked Daniel in the eye. "And as you know, Scott's forty-second birthday is next week."

"Now, Joyce," Bill chuckled, "if you ask me, it's crazy to give away a fortune like this just because you have some absurd idea in your head."

"Crazy or not, how can I take a chance with Scott's life?" Ms. Evans asked quietly.

Bill's face turned suddenly angry. "We're wasting time here! Get that gold and no one will be hurt."

"All right then," Ms. Evans pleaded, "let the kids go now!"

"Don't worry about them," Daniel assured her. "I plan to keep them company until Dad is well on the road to Quesnel." He pulled a two-way radio from his vest pocket. "Good thing we brought these little gadgets along. Cell phones are useless in these stupid mountains. Ah-ah-ahchoo!" He tucked the radio under his left arm and fumbled for a tissue. "Can't wait to get back to civilization!"

During all this talk, Katie and Sheila eased away from the mine shaft. Ms. Evans walked over to them. "Please, girls, hand me the boxes. I don't want any of you to get hurt."

Sheila did as she was asked. Ms. Evans turned to Katie, who hesitated, then did the same.

"Thank you for trying to help," Ms. Evans said sadly. She handed the two boxes to Bill, who put them into his sports bag and slipped the strap over his shoulder.

He placed a heavy hand on the back of her neck. "Shall we go?"

The two were soon swallowed up by the forest. Katie started to follow.

"Stop right there!" Daniel yelled. Shifting the tissue to his left hand, he reached into his pocket and came up with a bright yellow plastic object. It was shaped like a small, short-barreled gun and he pointed it at Katie. "Don't make me use this." he warned.

"A toy gun?" Katie asked.

A shock of fear ran through Rusty. He knew exactly what it was because his parents kept one just like it in the emergency kit on their boat.

"Flare gun," Daniel growled, "loaded and ready to fire."

"He's not kidding," Rusty said. "One shot from it could set you on fire!"

Halfway between the mine shaft and the edge of the forest, Katie stopped. "So, Daniel, what's your father planning to do with Ms. Evans?"

"Don't worry. Everyone cooperates, no one gets hurt."

"But how can you do this?" Sheila asked. "Aren't you Scott's friend?"

Daniel's attention shifted to Sheila. "You think Scott believes that ridiculous curse? He figures fishing with Brandon is more important than traipsing across the country on a fool's errand."

"But what if it's true?" Sheila asked. "What if your best friend dies next week? How will you feel then?"

Daniel growled, blew his nose and tossed the tissue on the ground. He didn't notice Katie take another step toward the forest. "I gottta tie you kids up so I can meet my father on the highway."

"On your motorcycle?" Rusty asked.

Daniel ignored him and slipped a coiled rope from his shoulder. Katie took one more step away, but this time he noticed. "You! Get back here!" he shouted.

Katie studied Daniel, hesitated between running away and doing as he said.

On the opposite side of Daniel and slightly behind him, Rusty didn't think the man would actually use that flare gun, but who knew? *The lure of gold,* he thought, *it makes people do terrible things.* More than anything, Rusty wanted to turn and run for his life, but he knew he couldn't desert Katie and Sheila. And Ms. Evans still needed their help. It was up to him. He had to do something, now, while Daniel's attention was on Katie and Sheila.

Cautiously, soundlessly, Rusty took one step and then another toward Daniel. Less than two steps away, Rusty knew what he had to do. He had one chance and he must not blow it. So he needed to pay attention and wait until the moment was exactly right. *The best defense is the element of surprise.*

Rusty stopped breathing. Took one more step.

"I'm warning you, girl!" Daniel yelled at Katie.

Rusty was now in the perfect position. He nodded at Katie, who said in a loud voice, "All right, you win." and moved toward Sheila.

"You do realize this is kidnapping and unlawful confinement?" Sheila asked. "You'll spend a long time in prison when they catch you."

"Ha! No way we'll get caught. Once we're outta here, you don't have a speck of proof." He glanced from one to the other of the girls. Then, as if suddenly remembering Rusty, he started to turn.

Now! Rusty thought. He took a deep breath, clutched his walking stick firmly in both hands, raised it high above his head and slammed it down, as hard and as fast as he could, on Daniel's wrist.

"YEE-OW!" Rusty and Daniel both screamed together.

A sharp pain shot through Rusty's sore hand, so unexpected he almost dropped the stick. He was aware, though, that the flare gun leapt from Daniel's grasp and landed on the loose gravel above the shaft. It skidded toward the opening.

"AIHHH!" Daniel bellowed and charged after it.

The last thing Rusty saw as he ran was the gun disappearing over the edge. An angry scream and a whoosh of falling gravel rang in his ears as he crashed through the forest behind Sheila and Katie. They didn't stop running until they reached the Richfield Trail.

"We'll never catch up to them!" Rusty gasped. "They're way ahead of us!"

"We will," Katie said. "Bill is a mess! He couldn't run if his life depended on it. They can't have gone far yet."

"What about Ms. Evans?" Sheila asked. "What do you think he'll do with her?"

"I don't know, but I don't think he'll hurt her so long as she cooperates. And she won't cause any trouble if she thinks we're with Daniel. So we need to catch up to them before Daniel catches up to us."

"But he fell into the mine shaft." Rusty shuddered. "How could he follow us?"

"No way he could fall down there." Sheila said. "It's way too narrow for the size of him. He won't be far behind us!"

17

Outsmarting Outlaws

A light rain started falling as they reached the bottom of Richfield Trail and could see down Barkerville's main street. A few tourists scuttled back and forth, but there was no sign of Bill and Ms. Evans.

"I can't believe this," Katie said. "We're way faster than them. Where could they be?"

Katie and Sheila started into town, but Rusty lagged behind. He wondered how Bill expected to walk through the busy town and the Visitors' Center, where the security office was located. For sure Ms. Evans would speak up when she believed her son's life was at stake. Or would she keep quiet to protect the kids?

He hardly noticed the miner's cabin to his right, but stopped abruptly at the start of a narrow trail on the left. Although he had not been on it yet, Rusty knew this was the Barkerville View Trail. Something white fluttered in the breeze, caught in tall grass. A tissue? "Hey!" Rusty called. "Hey, come back!"

In three steps he reached it and snatched it up. Not a tissue.

"What, Rusty?" Katie asked.

"Look! A white handkerchief. Ms. Evans left us a clue."

Katie studied the dirt path winding up into the trees, "Where does it go?"

"Along the ridge above town, past the Visitors' Center and all the way to the parking lot."

"Let's go!" Katie said.

They hurried up the trail, which zigzagged around trees and offered glimpses of the streets below. They had not gone far before a loud, wheezy cough filtered back through the woods.

"That's him." Rusty whispered.

"Now what?" Sheila asked. "How do we stop him?"

"I don't know," Katie admitted.

"Wait," Rusty pressed his fingertips to his forehead, "I'm getting an idea." He quickly outlined his plan, the girls offered suggestions, and they were ready. They ran along the trail until they saw Bill, his hand resting on Ms. Evans' shoulder.

"Bill! Ms. Evans!" Katie cried. "Help! There's been a terrible accident!"

Astonished, Bill swung around. "What are you kids doing here?"

"It's Daniel!" Rusty said breathlessly. "He fell into the mine shaft!"

Bill's face went white. "What? Is he hurt?"

"Well, it *is* a long way down," Katie said.

"With *huge*, jagged rocks at the bottom," Sheila added.

Bill slapped his hand against his forehead. "I knew we should never have done this! What was I thinking?"

"He needs help," Sheila said. "We should get the security guards and call an ambulance."

"Yes. Yes, you're right. Hurry!" Bill looked totally deflated.

"I told you that gold is cursed," Ms. Evans said. "Here, hand it over and I'll take care of it while you get help for your son."

Bill couldn't get rid of it fast enough. He shoved the sports bag at Ms. Evans and took off along the trail.

"The more people who hear about this gold the better," Ms. Evans said as they followed. "I'm going to call every newspaper, radio and television station I can think of. You kids will be famous."

Rusty gulped. Sheila looked horrified.

"The thing is," Katie explained, "we kind of don't want Gram and GJ to know."

"Oh." Ms. Evans thought for a minute. "Yes. I understand. They do worry about you, don't they?"

Bill's breathing became more and more labored, but he pushed on just ahead of them. At last the trail began to swing down toward the north end of town. Rusty looked over the roof of Saint Saviour's Church to the street in front of it. *Oh, man!*

Limping through the rain was a dirty, disheveled man with a crooked white beard and a hat pulled low over his eyes. At the rate he was going, they would all arrive at the Visitors' Center at the same time! Rusty tapped Katie's shoulder and pointed. Her eyes widened. "Psst!" she whispered, and Sheila glanced back. Occupied with their own concerns, both Bill and Ms. Evans kept walking.

"We've got to stop him," Katie whispered.

"But how?" Sheila asked.

"Hey, look!" Rusty pointed.

Head down against the rain, a woman darted out of an alley next to a stagecoach unloading passengers. Her full skirt swung back and forth like a bell, and the dark cloud of her hair, wet now, sank around her shoulders. She was on a collision course with Daniel.

As they scrambled down the bank, they formed a plan.

Phyllis stopped short as they approached her.

"Hey!" Rusty called. "Did you see him?"

Phyllis frowned. Her gray eyes bored into Rusty's. "See whom?"

"Three Finger Evans," Katie whispered. "Look! There he is!"

"He must be returning the gold!" Sheila said.

Phyllis looked. Her jaw dropped. The man wore the clothes of an old prospector. His shirt and vest were coated in dust, quickly turning to mud; his pants were ripped and his boots scuffed and dirty. His crooked beard was streaked with brown as he limped toward them, a rope coiled over his shoulder, his head down, seeing no one.

"Three Finger!" Phyllis shrieked. She ran over, stopped in front of him and gazed up in wonder. "Is it true? Are you real, then?"

Several of the passengers from the stagecoach heard Phyllis and looked over. "Come see!" Rusty called. "This is a brand-new demonstration. Watch what happens!"

Daniel glanced up, confused. "Who are you? What are you talking about?"

Phyllis reached out a long, scrawny finger and poked him on the chest. "Amazing! You feel so real. Tell me, Three Finger, do you have the gold?"

His eyes widened. "How do you know about the gold?"

"Because it doesn't belong to you, you know. You stole it and I hope you're planning to give it back."

"Look, lady, I don't know who..." He glanced around nervously. That's when he spotted the kids. "You!" he bellowed. "I should have taken care of you when I had the chance!"

"Now, Three Finger," Phyllis said, "let's not have any threats. You know you'll never rest in peace if you can't behave nicely."

"And just look at you," Katie said. "You're a mess. You really should think twice about threatening us."

"Right," Sheila added, "we're tougher than we look."

"And besides," Rusty pointed out, "all these nice folks are watching you."

Daniel growled under his breath. Then he looked down the road and cursed out loud. Rusty turned in time to see Bill entering the Visitors' Center with Ms. Evans right behind him. "Wait!" Daniel called, but they didn't hear. He limped after them with Phyllis close at his heels.

"You really must watch your language, Three Finger. We don't appreciate swear words in Barkerville."

Rusty, Sheila and Katie followed at a distance.

They huddled outside the Visitors' Center. "What now?" asked Sheila.

Before anyone could answer they heard GJ call, "Hey, there you are!" He and Gram hurried to join them.

"What luck! We just got back and thought we might have trouble finding you."

"Look at you three!" Gram said. "You're soaking wet! And you must be starved. You know, we've been thinking about lunch at the Lung Duck Tong Restaurant all the way back from Quesnel."

"So, let's go already!" GJ said and led the way down the street.

When they finally returned to their campsite, they found a note taped on the trailer door. Gram read it aloud:

Dear Friends:

I'm so sorry to miss dinner with you but something came up and I must get home as soon as possible. So I'm making a start this afternoon. I'll write my phone number below, please call me a week from today. I value your friendship and hope we can meet again.

Thank you all so very much,
Joyce Evans

"That's odd," Gram said. "What is she thanking us for? We didn't do anything."

GJ winked. "I expect a morning with these three was enough to make her run for her life. She's probably just grateful to get away and too polite to say so."

Rusty glanced at the girls. They looked as disappointed as he was to hear Ms. Evans had gone. He wondered if she managed to clear Eng Quan's name. Would her son safely reach the age of forty-two next week? How would they ever find out?

"Come on inside where it's warm and dry," GJ suggested, unlocking the door.

"Can we go for a bike ride first?" Katie asked.

"In the rain?"

"It has almost stopped," Katie pointed out, "and we really need some exercise."

"Or we'll be awake half the night," Rusty added.

"In that case, go," GJ laughed, "but come right back if it starts pouring again."

They followed Katie, who turned left out of the campsite. "Where are we going?" Sheila wanted to know.

"I want to see if Bill and Daniel are still here."

Ms. Evans' campsite was empty, so they rode in and hopped off their bikes near the picnic table. Through the trees, they could see the white van directly behind, but there was no sign of life around it.

"At least they aren't following her," Rusty said. "I wonder what happened."

Just then a small red car pulled into the campsite, the driver's door opened and a man stepped out. "Hi, kids!" he called. "It's good to see you again."

As the man walked toward them, Rusty recognized him as one of the security guards, the one named David Eng. What was he doing here?

"I had hoped to find Ms. Evans because I want to compare notes."

The kids stayed by their bikes while David Eng settled on the picnic table, his boots on the bench seat.

"What notes?" Katie asked.

"Notes about our ancestors," Eng replied. "You see, for all these years my four-times-great-uncle, Eng Quan, has been considered a criminal and his father has been accused of placing a terrible curse on the Evans family. I came to Barkerville hoping to learn the truth."

"There was a curse," Rusty said. "Ms. Evans came all this way to break it."

Eng shook his head. "Coincidence perhaps, or an initial fear that caused the curse to come true for Three Finger and his son. I expect Three Finger fell into a gulch somewhere, or was tossed in by those angry miners. Many men met a similar fate in those days."

"What about Eng Chung? What happened to him?"

"My family has a letter to my great-great-grandfather from his brother Eng Chung. It states Eng Chung's belief that Three Finger Evans purposely left that gold pouch under his stairs to cast suspicion on Eng Quan. The young man was not liked by the white miners because he complained about the poor treatment Chinese miners received in Barkerville. When the pouch was found, Eng Chung advised his son to run away before he could be arrested. After Eng Chung heard news of Eng Quan's death, he did not live much longer himself."

"What about the curse on Three Finger and all his first-born sons?"

"Although it is possible, and some say that an apothecary such as Eng Chung would know how to concoct such a curse, as I say, I personally don't believe in such things and there is no mention of it in his letter."

"But, just in case, did Ms. Evans manage to clear Eng Quan's name?"

Eng smiled and got to his feet. "That she did." He shook hands with each of them. "I want to thank you," he said. "Ms. Evans didn't say so, but I suspect you were a big help in all of this." Before getting into his car, Eng called, "Be sure to listen to the six o'clock news!"

When his watch finally said 6:00, Rusty asked, "Can we listen to the news?"

Gram and GJ exchanged surprised glances. GJ got up and switched on the radio to CBC.

There was a lot of news before they heard it: "A fortune in gold has been discovered in an abandoned mine shaft near British Columbia's historic gold-rush town of Barkerville. After 136 years, a mystery has been solved and an ancient wrong put right. Ms. Joyce Evans, relative of the original Three Finger Evans who stole the gold from several mines, says she is happy it has been returned at last. She wants the world to know that Eng Quan, the young Chinese man originally suspected of the thefts, was completely innocent. The gold will be used to restore and maintain the historic site for years to come.

"Meanwhile, two Ontario men have been taken in for questioning on suspicion of the kidnapping of Ms. Evans and attempted theft."

GJ switched off the radio. "That's incredible!" he said. "All this happened right under our noses and we knew nothing about it."

Gram glanced suspiciously from Katie to Rusty to Sheila.

"Amazing." Rusty grinned.

"Hard to believe," Katie agreed.

Sheila nodded. "Maybe that's why she left early."

One week later they stopped at Mount Robson Provincial Park. With the huge snow-covered peak towering above them, they clustered around a pay phone. Gram made the call. Rusty fidgeted, the girls looked worried.

"Joyce! Yes, it's Lynne Sampson calling. How are you?"

Rusty watched Gram's face and was relieved when it broke into a smile.

"Oh, that's wonderful! Certainly. Well, we do have until September, but Ontario is so far away. Yes, he is." Gram passed the phone to Rusty. "She wants to talk to you."

"Hello?" He heard laughter in the background.

"Rusty! Wonderful news! We're having a party at my new townhouse. It's my son's forty-second birthday today!"

"That's good." Rusty was relieved and happy for her and wished he could think of something more exciting to say.

"And Rusty? My grandson Brandon is here. I told him about you—not everything, you understand, and don't worry, I don't intend to tell anyone the whole truth. You, Katie, Sheila and I are the only ones who know what really happened."

"Thank you."

"No, Rusty, it's you and the girls who have my eternal gratitude. You're true heroes in my book."

Rusty couldn't think of an answer, so he was relieved when Ms. Evans continued. "Anyway, Brandon wants to meet you. If you get anywhere near Cornwall this summer, come and visit us."

"That would be fun," Rusty said.

While Ms. Evans talked to Sheila and Katie in turn, Rusty gazed up at the massive, snowy mountain peak that dwarfed everything for miles around. Tomorrow they would drive through Yellowhead Pass and into Alberta. He wondered if the rest of their trip would be anywhere near as exciting as their visit to Barkerville.

Spirits of the Cariboo

Barker, William. Billy Barker arrived at Williams Creek in August 1862. He is thought to have been a sailor who jumped ship in Victoria after being lured by tales of gold. Short, bowlegged and with a bushy salt-and-pepper beard, Billy Barker always wore his sailor's belt, and for good reason. The punishment for deserting ship was death. However, if a man kept just one article of his sailor gear with him, he was not considered a deserter but merely AWOL. Inspired by Ned Stout, Billy Barker dug below the canyon near a rock outcrop where he estimated the creek had once run. Other miners joked and laughed as Barker dug deeper and deeper without finding a trace of gold. They stopped laughing when he hit paydirt. A one-square-foot shovel load yielded $1,000 in gold. Although Barker became a very rich man, he lost every penny and died in poverty.

Barkerville. Shops, saloons and houses quickly rose up around Billy Barker's claim to create the town of Barkerville. But every spring, when the mountain snows melted, Williams Creek overflowed into the streets. The problem was made even worse by miners who diverted the creek in their constant search for gold.

The people of Barkerville were resourceful, though. They built every house and shop on stilts to let the spring floods flow below their floorboards. A little advance planning might have been in order, however, because every building was at a different height and so was the boardwalk in front of it, which made walking somewhat hazardous. Stairs from the boardwalk descended to a muddy road where cattle, pigs and horses added their contributions to the mucky mess.

Most of the miners lived outside of town in tents, dugouts or lean-tos. Some built tiny, one-room log cabins. Fireplaces were made from rocks cemented together with clay. Thousands of trees were chopped down, leaving only stumps behind, and the barren hills were soon covered with tents and shanties.

Barnard, Francis Jones. On April 14, 1861, Barnard was a purser on the *Fort Yale*, comfortably seated in the steamboat's dining room. Suddenly he was blown straight up into the air and landed outside on the railing of a sinking ship. The *Fort Yale's* overheated boiler had exploded, and many on board were killed. Luckily for Barnard, he was soon plucked out of the water by local Natives. It might be while he was flying through the air, or perhaps as he was dragged helplessly downstream, that Barnard came up with the idea of starting an express business on dry land.

Barnard began by delivering letters and newspapers between Victoria and Barkerville and later ran a successful wagon service on the Cariboo Wagon Road. Ten years after his amazing flight, Barnard had another run-in with a boiler. This time he purchased two "Patent India Rubber-tired Road Steamers" to carry freight between Yale and Barkerville. Stacks of wood were left along the roadside to fuel the first of these cumbersome machines, but the steep mountain roads altered the boiler's water level so drastically that the boiler became dangerously overheated. After three days, Barnard's road steamer gave up the struggle at Jackass Mountain.

Begbie, Matthew Baillie. The British government selected Begbie, a lawyer, to be the judge responsible for bringing law and order to its brand-new colony of British Columbia. Sometimes on foot, sometimes on horseback, Begbie traveled his circuit from one community to another to hold trials wherever a crime occurred. Along the way, he often caught his own food by fishing and hunting. During his travels, Begbie made excellent maps of the trails for others to follow.

From the start, Begbie had a reputation for treating all suspects fairly. His firm justice kept the Cariboo gold rush much safer than the lawless California gold rush had been. Even so, to be on the safe side, Begbie acquired the habit of traveling with a bodyguard, a huge and fierce Native man who wielded a hunting knife and a bow and arrow.

Although he became known as "The Hanging Judge," Begbie only gave the death penalty when he felt it was necessary.

Cameron, John. Cameron, his wife, Sophia, and their infant daughter set out from Cornwall, Ontario, by ship in 1862. They arrived in Victoria penniless and with a very sick child. The little girl died, but Cameron and a grieving Sophia continued on to the Cariboo. They arrived a few days after Billy Barker.

Cameron and his partners staked ground downstream from Barker and started digging. In October, shortly before Sophia, who hated the Cariboo, died of typhoid, she extracted a promise from her husband. Two months later, Cariboo Cameron struck it rich.

Early the following spring he loaded his wife's coffin on a sled and, with a few helpers, dragged it all the way to Victoria. Often they lost control in ice and snow, and the heavy coffin went shooting down slopes, only to be dragged laboriously up again. Cameron later accompanied the coffin, filled with whiskey to preserve the body, back to Cornwall. His promise to Sophia had been kept.

Chinese laborers. Within a span of two weeks in 1860, more than 700 Chinese men arrived in the Cariboo. Most of them came directly from China, but some had taken part in the earlier California gold rush and moved north to join the Cariboo gold rush.

Chinese miners were treated badly, partly because they were willing to work for less pay than white miners. The Chinese men often moved in to work mines previously abandoned by white miners. Chinatowns thrived in Victoria, Quesnel and Barkerville. On the steep slope above Barkerville, the Chinese built terraced gardens to provide themselves and the town with fresh vegetables.

Dietz, William. Along with Michael Burns and Vital La Force, Dutch Bill Dietz pushed north from the goldfields at Antler Creek in late 1860. The ground was covered by snow when Dutch Bill tested near a bare rock outcrop at the side of a creek and found $1.00 of gold to the pan. The creek was named Williams Creek after him.

Hurdy Gurdy Girls.

This was the name given to young girls brought north from San Francisco by Madame Bendixen. They were employed in the saloons to dance with miners and accompany them to the bar for a drink. The girls drank fruit juice and were paid fifty cents for every drink a miner bought.

The girls were originally brought to North America by a man known as "Boss Hurdy." Most of them came from very poor German families, and their fathers were given money for letting them go. The girls were then forced to work until their father's debt was paid back. However, this was almost impossible to do because the pay was so low.

Moses, Wellington Delaney.

Born in England, Moses traveled to California during the 1849 gold rush. He moved north when the California gold rush ended and the Cariboo gold rush was in full swing. In Victoria, Moses, a black man, opened the Pioneer Shaving Saloon, known for providing the first bathtub in Victoria. He then moved to Barkerville, where he opened his barbershop and placed an ad in the *Cariboo Sentinel* that promised "the restoration of hair in one week" by using his famous "Hair Invigorator."

Sometimes called the Black Barber of Barkerville, Moses became famous as the man who recognized a unique gold stickpin worn by James Barry. This led to Barry's arrest and subsequent hanging for the murder of Moses' friend Morgan Blessing on the road between Quesnel and Barkerville.

Stout, Ned. In the summer of 1862, Ned Stout had a plan. No claims were left in Richfield above the canyon, and no one had found anything worthwhile below the canyon, so he decided to prospect a gulch containing a stream that ran into Williams Creek below the canyon. Near the surface Stout found dull, waterworn gold, but when he dug deeper he came up with the more valuable bright, coarse gold. Stout gradually worked his way up "Stout's Gulch" and earned about $1,000 a day.

Mystery from History
Dayle Campbell Gaetz

**A thrilling romp through history and
present-day skullduggery**

While exploring near an abandoned oceanfront mansion, Katie, Sheila and Rusty stumble across a long-buried mystery and a present-day crime. Seeing themselves as amateur detectives, the three friends take on a case the local police department seems determined to ignore, and in the process they put their own lives in the utmost danger.

Spanning more than a century and covering a large chunk of the history of Victoria, the conspiracy reaches from Spanish pirates to the highest levels of the present-day police department. Intertwined with bloodthirsty pirates, Native legends, stolen gold-rush bullion and a lost diary, Katie, Sheila and Rusty uncover an international ring of art thieves and smugglers who are tied to the past in the most unexpected way.

Discounted by the police and eager to solve the case on their own, the amateur detectives have their lives threatened several times; they must use all their resources to outwit the thieves.

Mystery from History is a thrilling romp through colonial history and present-day skullduggery, with three likeable detectives. Seamlessly weaving the historical narrative with a contemporary story, Dayle Campbell Gaetz has written a story to please both crime and history buffs. In the spirit of Eric Wilson, *Mystery from History* is sure to delight and intrigue young readers.

JUVENILE FICTION

1-55143-200-5 $8.95 CAN $6.95 US

The best-selling author of a dozen books for young readers, **Dayle Campbell Gaetz** is a full-time author and creative writing instructor. She lives in Campbell River, BC.

Other books by
Dayle Campbell Gaetz

Mystery from History (Orca Book Publishers)

No Problem (Orca Book Publishers: Orca Soundings)

Living Freight (Roussan Publishing Inc.)

The Golden Rose (Pacific Educational Press)

Night of the Aliens (Roussan Publishing Inc.)

Alien Rescue (Roussan Publishing Inc.)

The Mystery at Eagle Lake (Quintin Publishers)

The Case of the Belly-Up Fish (ITP Nelson)

Spoiled Rotten (Maxwell Macmillan)

Tell Me the Truth (Maxwell Macmillan)

Heather, Come Back (Maxwell Macmillan)